Garfield's Apprentices Book 1

Leon Garfield has made a particular name for himself as a writer of stories for children set in the eighteenth century. He has been awarded the Carnegie Medal, the *Guardian* Award and the Arts Council Award, and his books have been translated into eight languages and have been adapted as television serials.

Leon Garfield

Garfield's Apprentices

book one

The Lamplighter's Funeral
Mirror, Mirror
Moss and Blister

illustrated by Faith Jaques

Piccolo Pan Books
in association with Heinemann

First published in Great Britain 1976 in three separate volumes
by William Heinemann Ltd
This edition published 1979 by Pan Books Ltd,
Cavaye Place, London SW10 9PG
in association with William Heinemann Ltd
© Leon Garfield 1976
Illustration © Faith Jaques 1976, 1979
ISBN 0 330 25617 3
Printed in Great Britain by
Richard Clay (The Chaucer Press) Ltd, Bungay, Suffolk

The Lamplighter's Funeral

to Jane

At half past after eleven o'clock (by the great bell of
Bow), of a cold, dark October night, a coffin came out
of Trump Alley, with six figures in white to shoulder it
and a river of fire to light it on its way. Smoke pouring
upwards heaved and loitered between the second and
first floor windows of the narrow tenements, so that
those looking down saw, as it were, a thick, fallen sky
dimly pierced by a moving crowd of flames.

'It's heathen,' said one soul whose parlour had filled
up with smoke. 'Why can't they go by daylight, like
decent Christians?'

Slowly, and with much jolting (the bearers were of
unequal height), the coffin turned right and lumbered

down St Lawrence Lane in the wake of the marching fire.

'I wish you long life,' said an old Jew to a coffin-bearer he knew by sight; and a little crowd on the corner of Cheapside uncovered as fifty lamplighters, all in white jackets and black cocked hats, filed across the road and turned into Queen Street with torches blazing and stinking the night out with fumes of melting pitch.

In accordance with old custom, they were burying one of their number whose light had been eternally put out two days before, in consequence of an inflammation of the lungs. One Sam Bold, lamplighter of Cripplegate Ward, having providently joined the burial club and paid his dues, was now being conducted with flaming pomp to his last snuffing place in St Martin's Church-yard. Although he had been a solitary man, such was the brotherhood of the lamplighters that any death among them made more than a small hole in the night; their yellowed faces were dull and sad . . .

One in particular looked sadder than all the rest, not from any extreme of grief, but because, having a chill himself and thinking too much of the fate of Sam Bold, he had taken a good quantity of gin to keep out the murderous cold air. The night had hit him hard, and he felt dizzy. Already the cobbles of Cheapside had almost overturned him; as he got into Queen Street he caught his foot against a rift in the pavement and went down in a shower of sparks and blazing pitch, like a comet of doom.

A crowd of street urchins who had been following Sam Bold's fiery progress to the grave, screamed with unseemly excitement while the lamplighters tramped

grimly on. Then one child – more perilous than the rest – darted forward and picked up the still burning torch. A slender, skinny-fingered child with eyes as round as hot pennies...

The torchlight lit his face so that it seemed transparent with fire and floating in the smoke. The fallen lamplighter gazed vacantly at the apparition; then, overcome with shame at his fall, tried to explain:

'Issa f-funeral ... muss go on. Respect ... feel awful...'

The child stared down.

'I'll go...'

'No ... no. 's not proper. Wouldn't be 'spectful ... Oh I feel awful..'

'I'll be respectful... reely.'

'You sure?'

'Cross me heart.'

'Take me – me jacket, then. Muss wear the p-proper jacket. It's the rule. And me 'at. Proper f-funeral 'at. Give 'em back later . . .'

The dazed lamplighter struggled out of his jacket; his hat lay in the street beside him.

''ere! P-put 'em on. Muss be 'spectful. Issa f-funeral . . .'

The white jacket engulfed the child and the hat finished him off so that the lamplighter had the weird feeling he had attired a ghost that had just departed, leaving the empty clothes standing, stiff with terror. A sleeve reached out and took up the torch again.

'I'll be respectful,' said the invisible child, and tipped back the hat sufficiently to uncover the seeing portion of his eerily solemn face.

The coffin had already passed on, and the deputy lamplighter had to scamper and run, with flame streaming, till he caught up with the funeral by St Thomas the Apostle and took his place among the marchers.

At last Sam Bold was laid to rest in St Martin's Churchyard and the deputy lamplighter acquitted himself with dignity and respect. He stood stock still amid the great crescent of fire that lit up the open grave and, with due solemnity after the black earth had thumped down, quenched his torch in the bucket provided – as did all the other brethren of the lamp – with the honourable words: 'A light has gone out.'

In the oppressive darkness that followed this general putting out, the company of mourners fumbled their way down Church Lane to where a funeral feast was awaiting them at the Eagle and Child. This was the custom; each man paid towards the coffin, and what was left over provided for meat, cakes and ale.

The Eagle and Child was an elderly inn that hung over the river like the glimmering poop of a ship that had taken a wrong turn and sailed among houses . . . One by one the mourners climbed up the wooden steps that led to the overhanging bay where the feast was laid out. Last of all came the deputy, not wanting to disgrace the occasion by hanging back.

The president of the burial club, who collected shillings at the door, held out his hand. For a moment there was a stillness in nature as to him who expected there was nothing given; the deputy did not possess a shilling. The president frowned, then observing the white jacket and cocked hat, took the occupant of them for Sam Bold's son. The dead man having been of Cripplegate ward and he of Bishopsgate, they had not been personally known to one another. For all the president knew, Sam Bold had a dozen sons, and this before him was the representative of them all. He withdrew his expectant hand and gestured the orphan through the door. One didn't demand a shilling off a bereaved child.

Inside the parlour, the talk was generally what it always is after a funeral: quiet, with a discreet cheerfulness breaking in; not everyone can be struck to the heart by one man's death. As the ale went down, spirits went up, and there was singing, of a gentle sort . . . nothing rowdy or quick; such songs as 'Sally in our Alley', or 'Over the Hills and Far Away'.

After a little while the deputy lamplighter joined in, not wanting to be conspicuous by keeping silent; his voice was high and singularly sweet. Several of the older brethren quietly shed tears, thinking, like the president, that there was Sam Bold's orphan, bearing up wonderfully. None liked to ask where his mother was, for fear of opening old wounds if, as was likely, she turned out to be dead.

At half past midnight there was a commotion on the steps outside, as of many feet struggling against incomprehensible odds. The president went to open the door and the lamplighter who'd fallen in Queen Street appeared in a dusty and confused condition. After greeting the company, he searched out his deputy and recovered his jacket and hat.

''ad a good feed, lad?' he inquired, gesturing towards the remains of the feast.

The lad, thin and bitterly ragged, looked up and shook his head.

'Not so much as a drop or a crumb,' said someone, not understanding the deputizing arrangement and still taking the child to be an orphaned Bold. 'It's only to be expected,' he went on. 'No appetite. Next of kin, you know . . .'

The new arrival – whose name was Pallcat – looked muddled. The child plucked him aside.

'I didn't like to say . . . I didn't have no shilling . . . And it was only till you came . . . I'll go now—'

Pallcat, not yet his usual miserly self, felt in his pockets for a coin.

'I don't want nothing,' murmured the child awkwardly. 'Reely.'

Instantly Pallcat took his hands out of his pockets.

'Wodger do it for, then?'

'I was sorry for you . . .'

Pallcat stared down disbelievingly.

'What's yer name?'

'Possul.'

'Possul? That ain't a name,' said Pallcat.

''s after St Thomas the Apostle, where I does odd jobs.'

Totally mystified, Pallcat scratched his greasy head, which reeked of the fish oil that supplied the lamps.

''ave a cake,' he said at length. ''ave a piece of pie and a thimble of ale. 's all right. I paid me dues . . . and I ain't up to eating meself.'

Possul gravely thanked his benefactor and drank and

ate. Then there were more songs and Possul obliged the company with 'While Shepherds watched', sung solo until he got to 'and glory shone around', when the company softly joined in, as became a congregation of lamplighters.

At half past one, the last of the candles supplied by the landlord of the Eagle and Child went out and the funeral party departed into the moonless night, pausing at the foot of the steps to shake each other by the hand and get their hazy bearings from the watermen's lights that still flickered and danced on the black river.

'Where d'you live, Possul?'

'Over Shoreditch way.'

'With yer ma and pa?'

Possul shook his head vigorously and Pallcat fancied he'd half smiled. (Queer, that, thought Pallcat for a moment.)

'I got rooms in Three Kings Court,' he said, blinking to clear his brain. 'Just back of Covent Garden.'

Possul gazed at him in admiration.

'Two rooms,' went on Pallcat, moved to a foolish boasting. 'You can come back with me if you like—'

The invitation just slipped out. Pallcat's heart sank as he heard his own voice oozing hospitality. He could have bitten off his tongue. He hoped Possul hadn't heard him . . .

'Don't want to be a trouble to you.'

'No trouble,' snarled Pallcat. ''s a pleasure.'

The journey back to Three Kings Court was full of corners and carpings, as Pallcat roundly cursed the lamplighters of those wards and parishes who'd been too dishonest to fill their lamps to last out the night.

'Issa sacred dooty,' he kept saying as blackness engulfed them. 'Issa Christian office to lighten our darkness. And it's a wicked 'eathen thing to give short measures and sell the oil what's left.'

Pallcat's drunkenness kept coming over him in waves; and whenever it went away he felt very cold and couldn't keep his eyes off skinny Possul to whom he'd offered a bed for the night.

Why, in the name of all the saints, had he done such a thing? It wasn't like him. What if Possul *had* helped him out and said nothing to the lamplighters about the shameful circumstances that had made it necessary? He, Pallcat, had fed him for his trouble. Surely that was enough? He glared at Possul whose face was bright with expectation. 'You ought to be on your knees and thanking me,' thought Pallcat, irritably.

The smell of ancient cabbage and trodden oranges stole upon the air as they neared Covent Garden. Pallcat had always lived alone, and had steadily improved himself by having no other soul to provide for. He worked hard, lighting his lamps at sunset and, thereafter, offering himself out as a link-man to light those who paid him the way home.

Such earning a living by shedding light in darkness gave him notions of great importance about himself; it was hard for him not to think of himself as some kind of judge, dividing light from dark – and choosing where and when to shine.

This, combined with natural meanness, made men say of him that, when his link went out, he charged for the moonlight – if there happened to be any about.

'Second floor back,' said Pallcat, as they came to the lofty tenement in Three Kings Court where he lodged.

His room stank so much of fish oil that the smell seemed to come out and hit the visitor like an invisible fist. Within there was a sense of bulk and confusion that resolved itself, when he turned up a lamp, into all the wild and tattered furnishings he'd bought between the setting and the rising of the sun. Tables, chairs, chests, commodes, pots and jugs, together with a quantity of glass cases containing stuffed birds and cats, were collected in meaningless heaps like the parts needed for the first five days of creation. There was also dust in plenty; it was not hard to believe that Pallcat himself had been formed out of it.

''ome!' said Pallcat, and, taking a taper from the lamp, lit another. The oil-stained walls appeared – between obstructions. Possul gazed at them in wonderment. Framed texts hung everywhere; some were burned into wooden panels, some were crudely stitched on to linen, as if by Pallcat himself.

'I AM THE LIGHT OF THE WORLD,' said one; 'HE THAT FOLLOWETH ME SHALL NOT WALK IN DARKNESS.'

'THE TRUE LIGHT WHICH LIGHTETH EVERY MAN,' proclaimed another.

'GOD SAID, LET THERE BE LIGHT,' hung over the foot of Pallcat's bed; 'AND THERE WAS LIGHT,' hung over the head.

'HE WAS A BURNING AND A SHINING LIGHT,' was propped above the fireplace; and 'LIFT UP THE LIGHT OF THY COUNTENANCE,' was nailed over a mirror that was tarnished like a disease.

'There's a couch in t'other room,' said Pallcat. 'You can sleep there.'

They slept away what was left of the night; they slept on through the grey and rowdy morning. Pallcat awoke some time after noon. Confused memories kept coming back to him, and he closed his eyes against the daylight that contrived to be as soiled as the windows. He recollected that he had company. Possul's weirdly transparent face, floating in smoke as when he'd first seen it, appeared before his inner eye. Then he remembered that Possul had carried the funeral light when he'd fallen by the wayside; that made some sort of bond between them.

He opened his eyes and gazed at his stuffed beasts which had been arranged so they might look back at him and reflect himself in their glass eyes. '"All is vanity and vexation of the spirit",' he mumbled; and pricked his ears.

The rooms were still. The thought struck him that Possul had already gone and, possibly, robbed him into the bargain. He crawled from the chaos of his bed and poked his head into the next room. Possul lay on the couch, breathing regularly. Being a child, he took sleep in greater quantities than a grown man.

Pallcat felt vaguely displeased; then he felt vaguely disappointed. He'd caught himself hoping that Possul, moved by the kindness and hospitality shown him, would have cleaned the room and prepared a meal while he, Pallcat, slept. But no such thing. The boy was ungrateful, like all boys. His angelic countenance and soft manners were things he'd picked up in the church where he'd worked; they were no more part of his deep nature than would have been a wig or a new hat.

He went out to get some food, determined to make the boy ashamed of himself for allowing a grown man to wait on him. When he came back, the boy was still asleep. Pallcat stared long and hard at his small, pale face, and had thoughts about shaking him till his teeth flew out; instead, however, he went into the next room and made a great deal of noise preparing to go out on his duties. He kicked against his oil can, dropped his wick trimmers and flung the lock and chain that secured his ladder to a banister rail with a heavy crash on to the floor. In spite of this, Possul did not wake up. Pallcat wondered if he was ill. He went back and laid an oily hand on the boy's forehead, and then touched his own; there was no great difference in heat. He bent down and blew gently on the child's face. Possul frowned, stirred and turned over with a sigh. Pallcat snarled and departed on his sunset task.

His lamps were in the Strand, stretching on either side from Charing Cross to St Mary's; also there were three each in Bedford and Southampton Streets, making four and twenty in all. High on his ladder, Pallcat tended them, filling the tins with oil, trimming the wicks, kindling them and giving the thick glass panes a dirty wipe before descending and passing on to the next.

From each lamp he took the greasy, burnt remainder and afterwards sold it to the boot-boys for blacking hats, boots and iron stoves. In this way he extended his dominion; he gave light by night and black by day.

In itself his task was humble, but when Pallcat was mounted up some twenty feet above the homeward hastening throng, and saw that the daylight was going, he felt as remote and indifferent as the kindler of the stars.

When he returned to Three Kings Court it was already dark; the kindler of the stars couldn't help feeling warmed by the thought of company. Possul was awake and sitting on the end of his bed; he hadn't so much as lifted a finger to clean or tidy anything. Pallcat put down his empty oil can.

'I'd ha' thought,' he grunted, 'you'd ha' done *something* – 'stead of just sitting and waiting.'

'Didn't like to,' said Possul, widening his peculiarly bright eyes. 'Might have done something wrong.'

'I left food out,' said Pallcat, baffled.

'Saw it,' said Possul. 'Didn't like to eat any, though. Just had some water.'

'Too idle to eat, even,' muttered Pallcat. 'You'll 'ave to mend your ways if you stay 'ere.'

Possul nodded and mended his ways to the extent of eating what had been provided. The lamplighter watched him half indulgently, half irritably; the boy ate everything, without asking if he, Pallcat, wanted any. He wondered how much nourishment it was expected of him to provide.

'If you are going to stay,' he said harshly, 'you'll 'ave to *do* something for it.'

Possul, his mouth so full that a piece of jellied veal was hanging out of it, looked up with bright, earnest eyes.

'I'll learn you,' said the lamplighter grandly, 'to be me apprentice. Now a lamplighter's apprentice is, very properly, a link-boy; that is, a nipper what lights the night folk their way 'ome. I done it meself – and I still do it; it's a 'oly thing to do. "And the Lord went before them . . . by night, in a pillar of fire, to give them light".'

'"The true light, which lighteth every man",' read Possul, off the wall.

'"Arise, shine; for thy light is come",' said Pallcat, handing the boy a length of tow that had been dipped in pitch.

'"I was eyes to the blind, and feet was I to the lame",'

23

said Possul, reading from a text that was still in the stitching stage.

'But not,' said the lamplighter, making for the door, 'without proper payment. Pitch costs money and tow don't last for ever.'

They went downstairs into the dark, cold court and walked to the Strand and along to the corner of Dirty Lane where there was a coffee-house with gambling rooms above. Here Pallcat kindled the torch.

'I'll show you,' he said, holding up the burning article so that his reddened eyes streamed from the sudden clouds of smoke.

Possul gazed at the lamplighter whose flame-lit countenance resembled an angry planet in the gloom; then his eyes strayed to Pallcat's lamps that winked in the obscure air down either side of the Strand. It took sharp eyes to make them out, they glimmered so feebly within the accumulated filth of the glass that enclosed them. Although they complied with the letter of the law and burned from sunset to sunrise, they mocked the spirit of that law and provided not the smallest scrap of illumination. If ever a world walked in need of light, it was the world under Pallcat's lamps.

'Light you 'ome,' shouted Pallcat, brandishing the torch before a gentleman who came stumbling by.

'No – no. I can see, thank you.'

'Fall in the river and drown, then,' said Pallcat to the gentleman's departing back.

He accosted several other passers-by, but none wanted light, so Pallcat damned them all; at the same time he shielded his torch lest a stray beam might have given an advantage not contracted for.

'D'you see? Like this! "Stretch out thine hand . . . that there may be darkness over the land, even a darkness which may be felt".'

At length, three gentlemen came out of the coffee-house. Their aspect was mellow, their gait airy.

'Light you 'ome?' offered Pallcat.

'And why not?' said one of the gentlemen, affably.

'A link-man with his spark!' said another, observing the boy beside the lamplighter. They all laughed and gave Pallcat lengthy directions to their homes.

Pallcat walked on ahead, holding the torch high; Possul took it all in, walking beside the lamplighter and occasionally raising his own arm in what he regarded as a professional way.

Presently Pallcat became aware that they'd attracted a non-paying customer, a wretched, gin-sodden devil who was lurching along, taking advantage of the free light to avoid the posts and projecting steps with which the streets were endlessly obstructed.

'Watch this,' muttered the lamplighter to his earnest spark. 'This is the way we does it.'

Pallcat took off his hat and, waiting for a sharp corner, whipped it before the torch, thus neatly plunging the stinking drunkard into an eclipse. There was a thump and a staggering crash as the wretch collided with a post and fell with a howl of pain.

'"Cast out into the outer darkness",' said Pallcat powerfully; '"there shall be weeping and gnashing of teeth".'

After that they were troubled no more and the three gentlemen, deposited in their homes, each gave Pallcat a sixpence for the guidance. Pallcat bit the coins and stowed them in a bag hung round his neck; then he and his apprentice went back to the Strand to see out the rest of the night.

Shortly before dawn, when Pallcat's torch was becoming superfluous, he and Possul returned to Three Kings Court. On the way the lamplighter pointed out those corners and alleys where pitch might be had, for a farthing a dip when a man's torch had burned through.

Before going to bed, Pallcat made Possul a bowl of soup, feeling, at the same time, that the boy ought to be waiting on him. But no doubt that would come in time. Possul was simple-minded; he needed careful training –

like a dog. And when all was said and done, he *was* company...

For an hour or so after Possul was asleep, Pallcat stitched away at his unfinished text, which was always his bedtime pleasure and task, and somehow made his world seem larger; then he too went down as the blaring sun came up and rendered his room a mad and dirty horror of too-visible confusion.

They slept the day through; Pallcat woke first and went out for food and more oil. When he returned he found Possul sitting peaceably on his bed, having done nothing but wake up.

'Tonight,' said the lamplighter peevishly, 'you'll work, my lad.'

Possul smiled contentedly and Pallcat could have clouted him with the length of tow that was to be his torch. The boy should have *offered*, instead of just waiting to be told, with his bright eyes going right through Pallcat like a pair of pokers.

'You go where we was last night. I'll go more towards Charing Cross. 'ere's a penny, 'case you run out of pitch before you gets paid. Remember what I showed you; remember about keeping your light for the lawful customers. Best take me cocked 'at; only don't scorch it.'

Possul, feeling immensely important – as became his occupation of link-boy – flamed outside the coffee-house on the corner of Dirty Lane. The warmth of his torch kept out the bitterness of the night, and his transparent-seeming face made a hopeful island in the black pool of Pallcat's hat.

'Light you home, ma'am?' he called out to a flower-cheeked woman who hobbled the street with eyes like cups of ashes.

'Shove off!' she said, and shrank from the damaging light.

Next, a pair of basket-women approached.

'Light you home, ladies?'

They drew near, smilingly shaking their heads.

'Just come for a warm, love.'

They held up their hands and drenched them in the heat of Possul's fire. The boy was nonplussed. Light he must not give without payment; but Pallcat had said nothing about warmth. On account of the basket-

women and several other freezing souls, Possul lost several likely customers.

All in all, he earned but a single sixpence that night – and then spent nearly half of it on fresh pitch for his waning torch. Pallcat was indignant when he'd got over his pleasure and relief at seeing Possul come back. Though he'd never have admitted it, he'd been haunted by the dread of Possul abandoning him as lightly as he'd joined him. He couldn't quite believe that Possul was real; that is, when the boy was out of sight . . .

He rated Possul soundly for his extravagance in pitch, and warned him to mend his ways. He sent him off to bed with – as the saying goes – a flea in his ear, which doubtless found company in Possul's horrible bed. Then he set about finishing his text and beginning a new one, especially for Possul: 'He that toucheth pitch shall be defiled therewith.'

Next night, with many warnings, Possul went out again to set himself up in business on the corner of Dirty Lane. The lamplighter, who accompanied him as far as the Strand, watched him flame his way towards the coffee-house with mingled feelings of suspicion and pride. The boy stalked along with such an air of self-importance that one might have supposed he was holding up the sun and moon and all the fledgling stars.

In truth, Possul had a soul no less than Pallcat; the sense of consequence given by being a minister of light had its effect on the boy no less than the man.

'Light you home, sir?'

'Take me to Clifford's Inn, child. D'you know it?'

''s off Chancery Lane.'

The gentleman nodded and Possul set off. Presently

a low noise in a cleft between two houses distracted him. He held out his torch. A woman and nearly naked child were huddled together in an attempt to get warmth from each other. The woman, half blinded by the sudden light, looked savage at the intrusion on her misery. Possul paused, as if to give his gentleman full benefit of the sight.

'Get a move on, boy,' he said. 'It's no business of ours in there.'

Possul withdrew the torch and left the cleft in decent darkness. A little while after, he stopped again. A legless beggar who squatted on a porridge pot and got about by dragging himself by fist and fingernail over the cobbles, squinted up from the entrance to an alley. Every detail of his misfortune was pitiless in Possul's leaping fire.

'Get along with you,' said the gentleman. 'Find something better worth looking at.'

So Possul looked and found a pair of lovers sitting on a doorstep. Furiously they bade him take his light away – which he did to his gentleman's protesting disappointment.

Just outside the gate to Clifford's Inn, a youngish woman was humped against a wall and crying. Possul lingered and his torchlight shone on her tear-stained face, revealing harsh bruises and dried blood.

'That's enough,' said the gentleman. 'When I want to be shown the miseries of the night I'll employ you again. Till then, my lad, keep out of my way.'

He gave Possul only threepence and dismissed him. The link-boy had two further customers that night, and, as if by design (though it was not so at all), he led them

likewise on pilgrimages through the horror and despair hidden in the dark.

Even as moths are drawn to a candle flame, so was every cruelty and misfortune drawn into the circle of Possul's torch. Or so it seemed. Consequently he got a bad name and each of his customers swore they'd never seek his light again. They'd sooner go home in the dark, relying on the lamplighter's feeble glimmers rather than the link-boy's bitter fire.

When he returned to Three Kings Court at dawn, he looked weary, but nothing to worry about. A night's work naturally wore a soul out. Pallcat took his apprentice's earnings, made him soup and packed him off to bed.

Next night, encouraged by his beginnings, Possul found other customers – and uncannily led them through similar ways, loitering his torch over all manner of luckless sights. Men crying in corners, dead children, thieves lit up in sudden, horrible terror. . . Human beings everywhere abandoning themselves to a despair that the darkness should have hid, abruptly seen in their crude nakedness.

Thus Possul's torch shed its light . . .

Sometimes it seemed that he took pleasure in what he saw; his face was always so earnest and bright. But no one giving him a second glance and catching his eerily solemn eyes could really credit him with so unnatural a pastime.

Although many of the sights he lit up would have been unremarkable enough by day, by night – picked out of the blackness like little worlds of total hell – they were vile and disgusting. The only explanation was that Possul lacked sensitivity and taste.

Pallcat of course knew nothing of this; Possul never talked much – and then only when spoken to. It never seemed to occur to him that he, Pallcat, had ears that liked exercise. Still, the boy breathed and ate so that one could hear him, and he was a living soul in the lamplighter's dingy lodgings. Pallcat even got a contrary pleasure out of feeding him for no thanks and being taken for granted as an ever-present father. If only, the lamplighter thought, he'd flesh out a bit and not look so shamefully skinny and pale. There was no doubt that, each dawn, when the boy returned, he looked whiter and more transparent so that Pallcat had the feeling that sooner or later he'd come back as plain bones.

The lamplighter kept his apprentice on the go for a week; then, on the seventh day, it rained so Pallcat told Possul not to stay out beyond midnight as no one would be about after that.

The rain was not heavy; it was more of a fine drizzle, a weeping of the night air that made the torch hiss and spit and give off smoke in thick bundles. Several gentle-men emerged from the coffee-house, but, having had their bellyful of the loitersome link-boy, waved his offers aside. In accordance with Pallcat's example, Possul wished them in the river. The curse, coming from his soft lips and attended by his bright, earnest gaze, seemed curiously terrible. Yet he uttered it more as if it were a charm to bring him the customers he lacked.

As if in response to this charm, a man came out of the coffee-house on his own. He'd had no experience of Possul so he was not driven to choose darkness instead of light. He was a huge elephant of a fellow, untidily dressed and wearing a frown as if he'd bought it as suiting his particular cast of features. He squinted balefully at Possul's fire.

'Light you home, sir?'

The man grunted ill-temperedly, searching his capacious mind and came out with: '"Take heed there-fore that the light which is in thee be not darkness".'

He sniffed and wiped his nose against the back of his hand.

'Well?'

'Yes sir. I'll take heed. Where to, sir?'

'Red Lion Square. D'you know it?'

'Off High Holborn, ain't it?'

'Thereabouts. Lead on.'

Possul lifted up his torch and went; the large man lumbered after. The rain, although not increasing, had soaked the streets so that the torch, reflecting upon the streaming cobbles, ran along like a river of broken fire. Bearing in mind his customer's strict injunction, Possul kept to the middle of the road and watched where his light fell. He could hear the irritable fellow quite distinctly, muttering and rumbling to himself like distant thunder over the trials of a bad night. The link-boy would be lucky to get a penny from such a man. At last they turned into Grays Inn Passage; the torch flickered across a bundle of rags heaped against a doorstep. As if unable to help himself, the link-boy paused. The huge fellow lurched and swayed to a halt.

'What d'you think you're doing, boy?'

'Nothing – nothing, sir. It's just me torch . . . shining, shining on—' He jerked the light apologetically towards the doorstep. The bundle of rags leaped out of the night; it contained a twig of a woman with arms and cheeks as thin as leaves. She was either dead or so close to it that it would have taken a watchmaker to tell the difference.

Possul remained perfectly still while his torch flames plaited themselves ceaselessly round the melting pitch and fried the soft rain. The huge man's complaints had died away into a heavy sighing; he swayed from side to side as if he found difficulty in managing his bulk.

He carried a stick – a heavy cudgel such as might have been used to beat off a footpad. He poked at the

rags with it. There was no response. Possul brought his
torch closer to the woman's face. Her skin was blotched
and covered with open sores that the rain had made to
shine. Her eyelids stirred as Possul brought the fire
closer still.

Suddenly a twist of blue flame – no bigger than a
finger – danced up above her mouth; then it vanished
with extraordinary rapidity. It was as if the spark of
life had been made visible, departing.

'Get back,' grunted the man, pushing Possul away
with his cudgel. 'She's full of gin. You saw it? That gasp
of fire above her lips. The torch set it off. Get away.
It's not for you and me to burn her before her time.'

He gave Possul another shove, swore malevolently at
the night – and bent down, so that every stitch of his

clothing protested at the effort. He picked up the gin-sodden, diseased creature as easily as if she'd been a frayed old coat; then he heaved her on his back.

'Move on,' he said to Possul.

'Where to, sir?'

'My house. Would you have me carry this unwholesome burden further?'

'What will you do with her, sir?'

'Eat her. Plenty of pepper and salt. Then I'll give her bones to my cat.'

The creature that was flopped across his back emitted a raucous moan.

'Peace, ma'am, peace. Presently you'll have comfort and warmth. Hurry, boy, hurry, before we're all poisoned by the stink of her gin.'

In a moment, Possul's fire broke out into Red Lion Square and cast the large man's shadow with its mis-shapen double back against the fronts of the stately houses; it seemed impossible for those within not to feel the dark passing. Possul himself, holding the torch, cast no such mark; the intensity of the light seemed to have eaten him up altogether; to shadow-fanciers, the lurch-ing monster with the grotesque hump upon its back was quite alone, save for a steadily marching fire.

Presently, the fire and the shadow halted. Then the shadow grew enormous and engulfed one particular house... Cautiously, and with solemn gentleness, the shadow's owner took off his hump and laid the tattered woman against his front door while he fumbled for a coin to pay the link-boy.

Why was the night suddenly so dark? He stood up and turned. The boy with the torch had vanished. The

square was empty and without light. He fancied he
glimpsed a flickering coming from the direction of
Fisher Street, which was some way off. It might have
been the light of a link-boy; then again, it might not.
The woman at his feet moaned again; he banged
ferociously and urgently on his front door. He looked
again towards Fisher Street, but the light had gone. He
shook his head as if to rid it of a memory that was
already faltering into disbelief. His front door opened,
but before he went inside, he stared upwards as if for
the sight of a new star. Nothing . . . nothing but blackness and rain.

Nor was it only from Red Lion Square that Possul had vanished; he disappeared from Three Kings Court, also. The night wore out, and Pallcat waited. Time and again he stirred himself and went down into the rain to search the maze of streets about Covent Garden. It was possible that Possul had got lost. Folk often did, round Covent Garden. He went along the Strand and wasted a whole torch in searching. Possul was nowhere to be found. He went back to his rooms. As he mounted the stairs his heart beat in expectation; he crept into Possul's room on tiptoe, almost as if he was frightened that, by making a noise, he'd scare off the fragile dream. He needn't have bothered. He might as well have tramped in with iron boots; the room was empty.

Next morning he went outside again, squinting pain-

fully against the cheap, all-pervasive light. He searched, he inquired, he scavenged in lanes and alleys; he went to the church where Possul had worked. The verger remembered the boy, but had not seen him for many days. Most likely he was dead; it happened sometimes, and mostly to the gentle ones. . .

Night came on, and, after tending his lamps, Pallcat renewed his search. He carried his torch through street after street, calling now softly, now loudly, for his apprentice. Every darkened alley might have concealed him; but the numerous stirrings and breathings in the night that Pallcat's sharp ears picked up, turned out to be such visions as Possul had lit up, visions of savagery and despair. These hateful and tragic images steadily burned their way into Pallcat's soul, as if the light he served had entered his breast and blistered his heart.

For two nights and days the lamplighter scoured the town; he scarcely dared return to Three Kings Court on account of the sharp pain of expecting, expecting . . . and then finding only filth, confusion and the emptiness of glass eyes. Possul had vanished, as if off the face of the earth.

At length he went down to the river, which he hated on account of its impenetrable blackness and sense of death. He asked of the watermen if they had seen, had *found* a boy? A thin boy with bright eyes and a transparent seeming face? They had not. But not to give up hope. Often corpses took days to come up and be caught under the bridge . . .

''e weren't real,' said Pallcat mournfully. He was in the parlour of the Eagle and Child, in company with two lamplighters from Cripplegate Ward. He had given up the river for the night.

On being prompted, Pallcat's companions recollected the boy at Sam Bold's funeral feast, but they did not recall Pallcat going off with him; one thought that the boy had gone off on his own, the other had no clear memories of the latter part of the night.

''e never talked much,' said Pallcat softly. ''e were just a – a *presence*. I *felt* 'im when 'e were there; and then when 'e went out I couldn't believe in 'im. 'e 'ad a sort of shining in 'is face. I do believe 'e were a spirit . . . I think.'

'What sort of a spirit?' asked one of the lamplighters, with interest. 'A angel, p'raps? Some'at of that kind?'

'No . . . no!' said Pallcat, with a flurry of indignation. 'A dream in meself. Something made up out of me mind. A spirit like – like—'

'Like gin?' offered the other lamplighter humorously.

Pallcat glanced at him, and the man saw with surprise that Pallcat's old eyes were bright with tears.

'It were a grand dream,' said Pallcat, half to himself. 'I wish I'd not waked from it, that's all.'

He stood up and walked to the window that hung over the river. He brooded on the blackness below, seeing his own face, irregular in the rippled glass, like something floating and drowned.

'I wish,' he whispered, 'I wish—' when Possul came in.

'*Where you bin?*' screeched Pallcat.

'Found this one with me torch,' said Possul, his bright eyes gazing at Pallcat hopefully.

Hanging on to Possul's back, much in the way the wreckage of a woman had hung over the large man's back in Red Lion Square, was an indescribably filthy and gruesome tot – a midget of an infant with a smear of a face and a crust of lousy hair.

'Got him out of the river by Salisbury Stairs. Been looking for his home. Ain't got one – like me. So I thought – I s'posed he'd make another spark?'

Pallcat did not speak, so Possul went on: 'I call him "Stairs", after what he fell in off. Can he come home with us?'

Still Pallcat did not speak. The thought of providing for yet another was looming large in his mind; nor could he rule out the possibility of others yet to come. He had seen a light in Possul's eyes such as no lamp had ever given. He could not put a name to it; all he knew was that without it the darkness would be frightful. He gave a little moan. He would have to clean up his rooms; no one else would. He would have to create order out of chaos; no one else would . . .

'I gave you a fine light, Possul,' said Pallcat hopelessly. 'And look what you have done with it. You must have come out of a winder, Possul; and that's where you'll end up. In a church winder, shot full of arrers. That's what 'appens to saints, Possul; and, all things considered, I ain't surprised. Come on 'ome – the pair of you.'

Possul smiled; and Pallcat wondered, not for the first time, which of them was being created in the image of the other?

Mirror, Mirror

to Jane

Between Glass House Yard and Shoemaker's Row lies Friers Street, where Mr Paris's premises occupy a commanding position on a corner. In the gloom of the November evening his shop window flares out extravagantly, as platoons of candles execute various dancing manoeuvres in flawless unison. On closer inspection, however, they turn out to be a single candle reflected in a cunning display of looking-glasses. Mr Paris is a master carver of mirror-frames; golden boys and golden grapes cluster round the silver mirrors and seem to invite, with dimpled arms outstretched, the passer-by to pause and contemplate himself.

Inside, in the dining parlour, the family are sitting down to supper: Mr and Mrs Paris – a handsome couple who will be middle-aged when it suits them –

Miss Lucinda, their young daughter, and Nightingale, the new apprentice.

Nightingale has not long arrived. He has scarcely had time to wash himself before sitting down to table. All day he has been tramping the streets with his father, a Hertfordshire joiner, and gaping at the multitudinous sights of the town. All in all, it has been a solemn day, what with the many unspoken leave-takings between father and son, the looks over the tops of toasting tankards of ale, the deep pressings of hands, the sentences begun and left half finished as the same melancholy thought strikes them both . . .

They have never before been parted; or at least, not for more than a day. But now the inevitable time has come. Ten pounds has been paid for the apprenticeship and Daniel Nightingale is to embark alone on the great voyage of life . . . as the village parson had been pleased to put it. Like all such voyages, it is to be seven years long, and the only provisions that the father might properly give his son to take with him have been the wise precepts he himself has treasured up and written down from his own seven years of apprenticeship.

Never come between your master and mistress . . .

Nightingale looks up the table at Mr Paris and then down the table at Mrs Paris; the husband and wife gaze at one another with identical smiles, as if each is the reflection of the other's heart.

Carry no tales or gossip between master and mistress, nor chatter with the servants of their private affairs . . .

A greasy girl comes in with a dish of mutton and a carving knife. She puts them both on the table with a glance at Nightingale that makes his blood run cold.

48

Look upon your master as another parent to you . . .

Nightingale catches Mr Paris's eye, but finds it altogether too slippery to hold. Mournfully he remembers his own parent; only a few hours ago he was 'Daniel, boy . . . Dan, dear . . .' Now that fond distinction has been shorn away and he is plain 'Nightingale'.

Perhaps now that I'm just a Nightingale, he thinks as a plate is set before him, I ought to sing for my supper? He smiles to himself, not having thought of many jokes before, wit in Hertfordshire being as thin on the ground as turnips are thick. Mr and Mrs Paris continue with their own smiles and the table presents an amiable aspect . . . with the exception of Miss Lucinda, the master's pretty daughter. She dislikes the new apprentice for no better reason than that he has failed to recognize her as the queen of the household. She knows it is every apprentice's ambition to wed his master's daughter and she cannot endure the notion of being a rung in someone else's ladder to the sky. She is not much beyond fourteen, with fair hair, fair skin and a general brilliancy about her that suggests she has caught some shining complaint from her father's wares.

'I hope and trust, Master Nightingale,' says Mr Paris, never taking his eyes off his wife, 'that at the end of your seven years we will all be as contented and smiling as we are now?'

The apprentice, caught with his mouth full, nods politely. At the same time, mournful thoughts of the day return. Seven years; seven long years . . .

After the meal, Mr Paris rises and shows Nightingale where he is to sleep. According to usage, the appren-

tice's bed is made up under the counter in the front room that serves as showroom and shop; thus if dreams come, they are more likely than not to be dreams arising from the day's work, so no time will be wasted. Mr Paris bids Nightingale goodnight and leaves him with a wax candle which he must be sparing with, as it is to last him for a week.

The apprentice mumbles his thanks and, when he is alone, prepares to say his nightly prayers. He is scarcely on his knees before the door opens abruptly and startles him. His master's daughter stands in the doorway. He has no time to observe her before she calls out:

'Nightingale! Catch!'

She tosses something towards him that glitters in the

candlelight like a speeding star. The apprentice is too surprised to do more than put out a hand that just touches the object before it falls with a crash to the ground. It is, or, rather, was, a looking-glass. Now it lies on the floor, shattered into silver knives and slices. Miss Lucinda smiles.

'You've broken a mirror, Nightingale. That means seven years' bad luck.'

'You slept well, lad?'

Mr Paris, smooth and glazed looking from his morning shave, came into the shop. The apprentice – hours of work, six until eight – had already taken down the shutters and swept the floor. Ordinarily as clear and truthful as daylight, Nightingale remembered his father's precept – *carry no tales* . . . He nodded in answer to his master's inquiry and said nothing of the sleepless night he had spent, caused by Miss Lucinda's grim prophecy of an apprenticeship that was to consist of seven years' solid bad luck.

He took breakfast with the family while the morning sun streamed into the parlour, enveloping Miss Lucinda and making her hard to look at. At half past seven he went to the workroom where Mr Paris's journeyman – an ancient craftsman with the head of a prophet and hands like the roots of trees – was already at work.

'Job,' said Mr Paris. 'This is Nightingale.'

The journeyman looked up from his carving and smiled at the new apprentice. Everyone in the household seemed to smile . . . excepting the daughter.

Nightingale, with the natural confidence of a good-looking youth, felt that sooner or later he would be able to melt her. His heart began to beat more easily.

'Come here, Nightingale,' said Mr Paris. 'Tell me what you see.'

The master drew a cloth from a handsome mirror that stood upon an easel as if it had been a painting.

'Look closely. Take your time, and tell me what you see.'

The apprentice, doing his best to reflect his master's smile, obeyed and looked in the mirror. A soft, blushing face that required shaving but once a week, beamed awkwardly back at him.

'Why, me, sir!'

'Indeed?'

Nightingale's heart sank as he heard Mr Paris's voice take on a decided edge. What *should* he have said? He felt as if he was suddenly standing upon nothing.

'Is it not very vain of you to think, Master Nightingale, that I should keep an image of you in my workroom? Why should I do such a thing? Who would buy it?'

The ancient journeyman sniggered; Nightingale went as red as a radish.

'Job,' said the master. 'Tell him what *you* see.'

Job, still sniggering, presented his own splendid countenance to the glass.

'I see vines, Mister Paris; and the fruits thereof. I sees naked little boys, what might be angels, a-buttressing the mitres. And at the bottom, finely 'graved, I see "Josiah Paris, Mirror Frame Carver. Friers Street. Blackfriars".'

'In a word, Nightingale,' said Mr Paris, 'he sees a *frame*. A well-carved frame. He does not see his own image, my lad.'

The journeyman smirked and went back to his carving, while Nightingale felt that his seven years' bad luck had begun with a bull's eye.

'In our line of trade,' went on Mr Paris, covering up the mirror, 'a craftsman – be he master, journeyman or apprentice – looks *at* a mirror, not *in* one.'

'Yes, sir. I see, sir.'

'A mirror,' said Mr Paris, expanding his thoughts and person at one and the same time, 'is nothing.'

'Yes, sir.'

'And yet it is everything. It is like life itself; it gives back only what is put into it. Smile – and you create a smile; scowl and you double the distress.'

'Yes, sir . . . I see that now, sir.'

'Human life is a mirror,' mused Mr Paris, as if his ideas were being reflected off mirrors inside his head. 'Thus the idle apprentice who gives his master only a tenth of his time, gets back, from life, only a tenth of its value.'

'Yes, sir. I'll always remember that.'

'There's much wisdom to be gained from mirrors and the framing of them, Nightingale. It is not for nothing that we say, when a man thinks deeply, he *reflects*.'

'He always does that,' chuckled the journeyman when the master had gone. 'It were the same with the last 'prentice and the one afore him.'

'Where are they now?' asked the third apprentice, sweeping woodshavings industriously. 'Didn't they stay out their seven years?'

The journeyman's chuckle faded into a remote smile and he bent over his work.

'It ain't for me to say. Carry no tales is a good rule for journeymen as well as 'prentices.'

Soon after nine o'clock, the shop bell jumped and Nightingale was summoned to assist his master. A tall, well-spoken gentleman had called to purchase a looking-glass for his wife. Books of patterns were duly consulted and several samples fetched out for demonstration of their quality. To Nightingale's surprise, the gentleman, who'd been overbearing to begin with, turned soft as putty and easy to please. Although he'd been as awkward as the devil about the patterns, the mirrors themselves had quite the opposite effect. He fixed on a simple oval and made his escape as soon as the price and delivery were settled.

Nightingale opened the door and bowed him out and into his carriage.

'Consumed with vanity,' said Mr Paris, handing his apprentice the pattern books and glasses to put away. 'That gentleman was eaten up with vanity. You saw how he couldn't bear to look closely at the mirrors? Only a vain man avoids his reflection so very particularly. He has such a fixed notion of his countenance that he will admit nothing that might disturb it. You saw what an ugly hooked nose he had? Most likely, inside his head, that nose was aristocratic. He had a hairy mole above his lip. Most likely he thinks of it as a rare ornament.'

Nightingale nodded in a bemused fashion and caught himself wondering if the radiant Miss Lucinda looked much in mirrors, and if she did was it a mark of modesty or was she contrary to all philosophy?

They dined at one: the journeyman in the workroom and Nightingale sitting down with the family after he had helped the greasy girl to bring out the dishes from the kitchen.

'I don't ordinarily take on a lad with an irregular cast of feature,' said Mr Paris, smiling down the table. The apprentice felt his cheeks grow warm, and he tried to absorb himself in the plate before him.

'Nor have you done so this time,' said Mrs Paris, glancing at Nightingale before smiling back at her husband. 'You really couldn't say he was wanting in countenance.'

The apprentice, though grateful for the compliment, felt his cheeks grow hotter; and Miss Lucinda's eyes seemed to be scraping the skin off his bones.

'In our line of trade,' said Mr Paris to the household in general, 'a dropped eye, a marred cheek, bad teeth or a bent nose are highly disadvantageous. The possessor of such a countenance would not be welcomed in this establishment. Bodily misfortunes we can tolerate, providing they are not exposed. Job has a fallen hip, and, I'm told, swollen knees. For my part, I've no objection to a wooden leg, even; if the stump be kept wholesome and clean. But the face must be as Caesar's wife—'

Here he acknowledged Mrs Paris with a peculiarly fine smile; '—the face must be above suspicion. We must be able to look in mirrors without awkwardness, without shame. A man with a defect of countenance, in such circumstances, might fall into a melancholia and go mad of it. In our line we must be able to endure and endure ourselves with equanimity. I don't say, with pleasure, but with equanimity. It cannot have escaped your notice, Nightingale, that we are a particularly fine-looking family?'

The apprentice looked up and saw his master's daughter sitting on her father's right hand. With every intention of being agreeable, he began to study her features with admiration and zeal. A look of sharp spite rippled across her face as if it had been a reflection in water, suddenly shuffled by a wind.

At eight o'clock the old journeyman took his day's wages and carried his magnificent head limpingly on his fallen hip and swollen knees out into the November dark. As he left, the old man asked the apprentice if he would care to join him for a glass of ale nearby? Reluctantly, Nightingale declined; he was weary to the point of faintness from his sleepless night and he ached for his bed.

He stumbled through the evening meal in a dull silence and afterwards begged to be excused from sitting with the family in the parlour. He was given permission to retire but not without a warning that his candle was to last out the week.

Thankfully he went into the shop and had scarcely taken off his coat when, as on the previous night, his door flew open.

'Nightingale!'

It was Miss Lucinda. Nightingale flinched in the expectation of something else being tossed for him to catch. This time, however, she had come on another errand.

'I want you to come and look at a mirror of mine,' she said remotely. 'It's upstairs, in my parlour. Come and look at it.'

The apprentice, swaying beside his bed as if he would fall asleep before falling down, said: 'Yes, Miss Lucinda.'

He believed that he must have made some inroads in her affections and that this was her way of showing it. He followed her upstairs, hoisting himself by the banister rails and counting them to keep awake. She led him into her little room where, in imitation of her

father's workroom, there was an easel on which stood a shrouded mirror.

'I want you to look in the mirror, Nightingale, and tell me what you see.'

He was to be tested again. He tried to think. What should he say this time? Should he praise the frame? Or, if she herself was reflected in the glass, should he praise her? What would please her most? Much depended on his words . . .

He stood before the mirror, preparing himself . . .

She snatched the cloth away. Nightingale shrieked aloud. A black-socketed skull grinned back at him! He trembled violently, believing for a moment, that he'd seen an uncanny portent of his own doom. Then he perceived that he'd looked, not in a mirror, but through clear glass behind which had been arranged the death's head.

Miss Lucinda laughed – and he rushed from the room in terror. Downstairs he lay on his bed, sobbing bitterly on account of the fright he'd had, on account of being the object of a hatred he could not understand, and on account of being parted from those who loved him. He felt he could never sleep again . . .

Next morning he awoke suddenly. Someone wild and amazed was staring him in the face. He leaped from his bed – to discover that a mirror had been set to confront him. He fancied he heard a sound of laughter in the passage outside.

He got through the day in a fog of bewilderment and unhappiness. The shop bell rang and rang; customers came and went; he bowed them in and bowed them out; he swept and tidied and stood stock still whenever Mr Paris chose to unburden himself of more wisdom than Nightingale thought ever should have been contained in a mortal head; and whenever he was alone, he crouched down behind the counter, held his aching head in both hands and wept like a child.

'I saw you crying behind the counter,' said Miss Lucinda, as she passed him in the passage. 'And all the street saw you, too.'

Filled with a new dismay, he ran back into the shop. High over the counter a mirror had been tilted so that everything was reflected outwards. He climbed up on a chair and took it down carefully, trying to avoid seeing the fear in his own face. After that he was cautious about every expression and every action; he could never know for certain whether he was being reflected, and watched.

Was it possible that the master knew what his daughter was doing? Perhaps he'd instructed her? Perhaps this was all his testing time? ·Perhaps it was like those ancient trials by fire and water to temper the spirit and make it worthy? Only his was a trial by mirrors . . .? 'A craftsman must endure and endure . . .' he murmured to himself as he sat, absorbed in such fanciful reflections, in the little necessary-house at the end of the yard. He had gone there more to relieve his mind than his body; and indeed, as his thoughts drifted, he did come to a kind of melancholy peace.

He raised his eyes as if to heaven; a shaft of light was shining through the ventilating aperture above the door. It fell upon a tilted square of silvered glass. Miss Lucinda's face was gazing down with a look of disgust and contempt. He cried out – and she vanished. He heard her jump down from whatever she'd been standing on; then he heard her feet pattering away.

He pulled up his breeches and hurried back into the workroom, feeling guilty and ashamed of being alive. He picked up a broom and began to sweep the shavings from round the feet of the ancient journeyman; then he went to fetch Job's beer.

The old man was working on a design of oak leaves and children's faces; patiently he tapped away with his mallet so that the bent gouge he gripped inquired into the wood like another finger. From time to time he laid his tools aside and set the frame against the mirror it was being carved for . . . and his marvellous prophet's head gazed back with a remote and dreamy rapture.

'Your beer, Mister Job, sir.'

The journeyman nodded. 'Lay it on the bench, Master Nightingale.'

The apprentice obeyed and looked again over Job's shoulder at the unfinished frame. The children's faces were sharply defined and were all exactly alike. They were Miss Lucinda . . .

Nightingale wondered if he dared question the journeyman about their master's daughter? He longed to ask the old man what *he* thought of her. Did she ever speak to him? Did she ever speak to anyone? Even her father and mother never seemed honoured with a word from her; nor, for that matter, did they speak much to her. Was she, perhaps, not their child? Or was she a mad child, suffered to roam the house and never checked for fear of provoking something worse than tricks with mirrors? Surely Job would know what she was?

The journeyman, without taking his eyes from the mirror, reached for his beer.

'Recognize 'em, Master Nightingale?'

'They're Miss Lucinda, ain't they, Mister Job, sir?'

'And a good likeness, don't you think? They was to have been angels. That's what they are in the pattern book. But I thought Miss Lucinda would be a nice fancy. It'll please the master. And that's what you and me's here for, Master Nightingale. Journeymen and apprentices alike must always please their master. Just as you aim to please your own pa at home.'

So she's an angel, thought Nightingale; and found himself left with no choice but to keep at his work and show, by all means in his power, that his chief aim in life was indeed to please his master.

After all, when he came to think about it all carefully, he wasn't so badly off. No one had clouted him; no one had injured him bodily . . . 'Country born and country bred,' he muttered with rueful philosophy. 'Strong in the arm and weak in the head. And what's wrong with that? Well, not weak, exactly, but good and solid. Nothing too fanciful. When all's said and done, there's no sense in thinking and thinking about something a country body can't hope to understand. And – and they say worse things happen at sea. So I ought to be thankful I've not been sent for a sailor! Besides, who knows but Miss Lucinda will come to respect me for holding my tongue about her tricks? Who knows, but I'll turn out the industrious apprentice yet and wed my master's daughter? They say it does happen . . .'

He pursued this line of comfort, with varying success, for the remainder of the day; whenever he passed Miss Lucinda he endeavoured to express in his smile, forgiveness for her cruelty and admiration for her beauty at one and the same time. On such occasions, she did not seem to see him. Then—

'Nightingale!'

Once more she was at his door and again demanding that he should come and look in her mirror. He sighed, and steeled himself for another look at the death's head. As he followed her he even prepared some sort of philosophical remark that he hoped would impress her with his worth.

'Look at yourself, Nightingale,' she said. 'Look at what you are.' She took away the cloth. A pig's head, still bloody from the butcher's axe, peered back at the apprentice.

He tried to laugh; but in truth he felt too sick and frightened to do more than imitate the grin of yesterday's skull. He stumbled out of the room and made his way back to his bed.

On the next day he came upon mirrors laid in different places; mirrors that caused him to fall headlong down a pair of steps outside the workroom, that led him to gash his forehead against an open door, that made him trip over a piece of wood that wasn't there and so to break a costly jug.

There was no mirror any more in the privy, nor was there one above the counter; but that didn't help. He couldn't be easy in his mind that they really weren't there. Indeed, he could not be easy in his mind about anything . . .

He found himself walking about the ill-lit house like one newly blinded – with hands outstretched, never knowing whether he was coming to a reality or its reflection. His chief hope was for the night; it was only in darkness that he could feel secure and be able to distort his face with weeping and anguish without restraint. Until that blessed time, he did what he could to wear the glazed smile of his master, his mistress and Job, the lame old prophet in the workroom.

When night did come, he was too sick and giddy in his brain to do more than nod when Miss Lucinda, like a white spirit, came to summon him to her mirror again. Wearily he climbed the stairs to the pretty little parlour.

A dead rat. He shrank away. Truly had the country
Nightingale flown into a forest of glass and thorn.

In the blackness of his bed he cried out against his
father's ambition that had sent him forth on so dreadful
a journey.

'I want you to be better than I am, Daniel,' he had
said aspiringly. 'I want you to be something more than
a humble joiner. You shall be a master carver and, God
willing, one day you will be carving cathedral pews and
screens and all manner of beautiful things. That's what
I want for my son.'

'And who knows,' mused his mother, 'but that some
day, like your father before you, you will wed your
master's daughter? It's the dream of every apprentice,
you know; and the reward for the industrious ones.'

'We are making a great sacrifice,' said his father.

'But no sacrifice can be too great,' said his mother, kissing him. 'Always remember that.'

Lying in a sea of tears, Nightingale remembered; and feeling his mother's kiss, wondered whether he himself was the sacrifice that could not be too great?

He knew there had been two other apprentices before him. Had they suffered as he was suffering? Had she hated them, too? This possibility gave him a crumb of comfort, and he fell to supposing they'd fled, no matter what the consequences, even though rebellion in an apprentice was reckoned a great sin. He tried to smile. Most likely they'd been town sparrows and knew better ways of the world than did a country Nightingale.

'I think you should know, Nightingale,' said Mr Paris, over the evening meal, 'that we are pleased with you.' As usual, he smiled down the table at his smiling wife, while on his right hand sat Miss Lucinda, the devil-angel of the household. 'I am writing to your father to tell him that we find you courteous and respectful.'

Nightingale smiled fixedly down at his plate. A week had passed and his spirit was broken as surely as the looking-glass he'd dropped on his first day.

He longed to cry out, to protest against the monstrous injustice to which he was being subjected. Every shame, every piece of spiteful humiliation that could be inflicted by mirrors had been daily visited on him; and nightly he'd been condemned to go to bed with an image of himself in a mirror that was no mirror, as something hateful and below contempt.

'Look at yourself! Look at yourself! Look at yourself!' Miss Lucinda commanded, standing in her pretty, blue-papered parlour, and uncovering, one after another, the framed sights of worms, a hanged man's head, a broken piss-pot with 'Nightingale' scrawled on it in black . . .

'I can tell you now, Nightingale,' went on Mr Paris, cheerfully, 'that when I brought you out of Hertfordshire, I had my doubts about country lads. One hears such tales of boys new to the town running after all manner of gaudy nonsense; worshipping the golden calf, one might say. An apprentice, my boy, must put his master above everything else. It's the only way to get through his seven years with honour and profit.'

Nightingale said, 'Yes, sir,' and went out to fetch his master another jug of ale.

•——≪≪≪≪≪≪ ❋ ≫≫≫≫≫≫——•

'Look at yourself, Nightingale. Look in my mirror. See what you are tonight.'

Miss Lucinda stood in her parlour, while the apprentice, already without his jacket – for she'd come to him late – swayed before the shrouded easel. Dully he'd been wracking his brains to imagine what she'd concealed this time behind the false glass? What hideous object could she have scavenged this time to frighten him with and to show him what he was?

'Look, Nightingale!'

She took away the cloth. The apprentice felt his head spin and his ears roar. Framed in the glass that faced him was – nothingness. Blackness, a bottomless pit . . .

The extreme shock of meeting with such utter emptiness overbalanced him. He felt himself begin to fall forwards, as if he was actually being sucked into the hole before his eyes. A black velvet bag had been placed behind the glass . . .

'Nothing,' she said. 'That's what you are now. Nothing . . . nothing.'

What would he be tomorrow, he wondered, as he half fell down the stairs? What was there on the other side of nothing?

It was a damp, misty morning with a cemetery chill on it; Job, who was afflicted with rheumatism in addition to his other bodily misfortunes, asked if the apprentice might be sent to Greening's in Glass House Yard to fetch a mirror that was cut and waiting? It would have been a cruel torment if he'd had to walk there himself.

'Nightingale?'

'Yes, Mister Paris, sir?'

'Can you find your way to Greening's in the Yard?'

'Yes, sir. Directly, sir.'

'Nightingale!'

'Yes, sir?'

'Check the glass carefully. They'll pass off rubbish if they can. No flaws, mind; no cracks in the silver, no spots of tarnish round the edges.'

'Yes, sir.'

'How will you judge, Nightingale?'

'I – I'll look at it . . . all over.'

'And what will you see, Nightingale? Yourself. Much good that will do us, eh, Job?'

The old man rubbed his knees and sniggered.

'The human countenance, Master Nightingale, is no yardstick for perfection; not even yours. Words, lad; that's what's needful. *In the beginning there was the Word*, and all that. Here, take this—'

He gave the abashed apprentice a card on which was printed, bold and black, something that might have been Hebrew for all Nightingale could tell.

'Just you hold it up to the glass they give you and read the letters clean and clear. Then you'll be able to see what's what.'

Nightingale put on his coat, took the card and set off. The very idea of going out after his distressful week revived him considerably; he felt, as he shut the shop

door behind him, that he was emerging from a peculiarly bad dream. However, once outside, this comfortable sensation was reversed by the mistiness of the morning that had the effect of rendering the buildings and street indistinct and much more dreamlike than the house he'd just left. Consequently he was quite unable to throw off the creeping uneasiness of what he might be shown that night in Miss Lucinda's mirror. What was that could lie on the further side of nothing?

He walked quickly, without particularly meaning to; the chill in the air forced him to be brisk and vigorous, even though he felt, as they say, distinctly under the weather. He reached Glass House Yard and found Greening's without difficulty.

It turned out to be more of a warehouse than a shop, with tall racks in which white-covered mirrors were stacked like huge, wordless volumes in a library for giants. The air in the beamed and boarded interior was brooding and pensive . . .

'Mirror for Mister Paris,' said Nightingale to a short, weaselish apprentice who appeared reluctantly from the obscure shadows at the back of the shop.

'Mirror for Paris!' shouted out the weaselish one to the shadows he'd just left.

'Third shelf along on the right. Got his name on it!' came a shout in reply.

The mirror, wrapped in white muslin, was brought down and laid on the counter.

'Sixpence on the clorf,' said the weasel, hopefully.

'I heard that!' came the shout from the back. 'There's nothing to pay and well you know it!'

The weasel shrugged his thin shoulders.

'Got to try and make ends meet,' he said amiably.

Nightingale smiled. The apprentice's attempt at sharp practice had been transparent enough even for Nightingale to see through. The other, not at all abashed, beamed over the counter.

'Givin' you a 'ard time, I see.'

'What do you mean?' asked Nightingale, uneasily.

'Paris and that 'orrible bitch of a daughter of 'is.'

'No such thing!' Nightingale shrank in terror from the temptation of pouring out his misery to a stranger. He smiled again, this time with the glazed smile that was the livery of his master's house.

'You look fair worn to the bone,' said the weasel, with interest.

'Stop gossiping and give him the mirror!' shouted the invisible one.

'Ain't gossiping. Just offerin' comfort to a fellow 'prentice in distress. It's Paris's new one.'

There came a thunder of large feet on bare boards and Mr Greening himself issued from the cavernous depths of his shop. It was not to be wondered at that he kept in the shadows; he was extraordinarily ugly with a monstrous nose that was afflicted with warts, like an old potato. He pushed his apprentice aside and laid his grey and silver stained hands on the counter.

'You always look as pale as a corpse, son?' he inquired, studying Mr Paris's new apprentice with small, bright eyes that resembled chips of glass.

'It must be the weather, sir,' said Nightingale, with a pang of alarm.

'How long have you been with Mr Paris?'

'Only a week, sir.'

'God help us!'

'I – I'm quite happy there, sir . . .'

'As the dying man said when the last drop of feeling left him,' remarked Mr Greening. 'Well, well, you'd best take the glass and be off.'

Eager to escape, Nightingale took hold of the wrapped mirror.

'Aren't you going to check it?'

Nightingale blushed and remembered the card. He produced it; Mr Greening nodded approvingly, unwrapped the mirror and obligingly held it up. Nightingale presented the card to the glass's silver face. The black words leaped out at him:

FOR NOW WE SEE THROUGH A GLASS DARKLY; BUT THEN FACE TO FACE: NOW I KNOW IN PART: BUT THEN SHALL I KNOW EVEN AS ALSO I AM KNOWN.

Mr Greening put the mirror down.

'All right, son?'

Nightingale nodded, but found himself staring into the air where the mirror had been. The words seemed to remain suspended in nothingness before him. He felt quite dizzy with trying to read them.

'Here!' he heard Mr Greening say. 'Fetch him some brandy and water. And mind – I know just how much brandy's left! Mirrors,' he went on kindly, reaching out a hand to guide Nightingale to a chair, 'can sometimes unsettle the strongest stomachs.'

Nightingale sat down. He couldn't imagine what had come over him. He felt faint and sick. He put it down to the strong smell of polishing oil that suddenly seemed to

be everywhere. Gratefully he drank off the brandy and water – which contained less water than might have been expected on account of the apprentice being generous with his master's property – and rose to go. His legs had gone like water . . .

'Sit still for a while. Wouldn't do to go dropping that mirror on your way back. Seven years' bad luck, you know . . .'

Nightingale nodded and shuddered; he looked up at Mr Greening whose nose now seemed so enormous that it filled Nightingale's world. The warts were like large, bald mountains and the tufts of hair that sprouted from the nostrils were like the forests of the night. Way, way above this fleshy landscape gleamed Mr Greening's eyes, as distant as the stars . . .

'I'm going to be sick,' said Nightingale.

'Got a bucket here,' said the weasel.

'Broke a mirror,' confessed Nightingale, after he'd brought up his breakfast, 'on me first day. That's what done it.'

'That's what done it.'

'She threw it to me,' said Nightingale, after a pause. 'And that's when it all started.'

'What started?'

'Things.'

'What things?'

'Mirrors . . . mirrors . . .'

'He's crying,' said the weasel brightly.

'Mustn't carry tales,' remembered Nightingale; and hiccuped.

'Won't tell a soul,' said Mr Greening sombrely. 'What about the mirrors?'

'Everywhere. Even in the privy. And the one upstairs. That's the worst . . .'

'Won't tell a soul,' said Mr Greening again. 'Why is it worst?'

So Nightingale told him . . .

What with the smoking of countless chimneys and, in particular, the dirty guffaws of the furnaces in Glass House Yard, the mist had condensed into a fog. Mr Paris's apprentice, emerging from Greening's, had immediately been plunged into the November breath of the town, which smelled as if all the inhabitants had belched after partaking of the same bad dinner.

He was carrying, in addition to the mirror he had been sent for, a wrapped box of about the same size as the mirror but some six inches deeper. It was heavy and seemed to grow the more so as he walked. However, the weight of it under his arm was as nothing compared with the weight on his heart.

He had betrayed his sacred trust. How he'd come to pour out all the details of his wretchedness to the ugly Mr Greening, he would never know. He believed that, somehow, he'd dozed off and talked in his sleep. He looked back towards the strange shop as if for an answer; but the establishment was already lost in the fog. He had a sudden idea of throwing the heavy box

away; he did not know what it contained and he was deeply afraid of it.

'It's a sort of mirror, you might say,' the weaselish apprentice had said, and grinned malevolently.

Mr Greening had warned him not to look in it himself. Under no circumstances was he to open it until she, and she alone, stood before it. He was to set it upon an easel, in a good light, and bid her look. The weasel had laughed aloud, and even Mr Greening had smiled as if in terrible anticipation.

'What is it? What will it do?' Nightingale had asked, trembling with shame over his betrayal and fear for the consequence of it.

For answer, Mr Greening had rubbed his grotesque nose and recalled the words on Nightingale's card.

'Then shall you know even as also you are known,' he'd said, and left it at that.

If the early morning had been dreamlike, the day had now grown up into nightmare; Nightingale wouldn't have been surprised if he'd awakened with a start to find himself under the counter in Mr Paris's shop. In the past he'd had dreams every scrap as convincing . . .

A fire came looping at him out of the thick air.

'Light you home, mister?'

The fog had brought out the link-boys with their torches like a plague of fireflies. Nightingale jumped, and stared at the thin, pale child who stood before him, holding aloft a flaming length of tow that really served no better purpose than to draw attention to the evil state of the weather. The light reached no further than a yard before it came back off the fog and bathed the link-boy in its glow.

78

'How much?' asked Nightingale.

''pends how far,' said the link-boy, blinking away tears brought on by his flaming pitch.

'Friers Street. Mr Paris's shop.'

''s only round the corner. Off Shoemaker's Row. Cost you a penny.'

Nightingale closed with the offer and the link-boy set off, miraculously weaving his way through a nothing that hid countless bulky somethings. Dazedly Nightingale kept his eyes on the streaming fire that superfluously added its own smoke to the atmosphere. He wished he'd got rid of the box before the link-boy had appeared.

'Nothing like a bit of fire for keeping out the cold,' said the link-boy, and offered Nightingale a warm.

Although the torch shed no useful radiance in any particular direction, there was no doubt that Nightingale found its presence a comfort.

'Friers Street,' said the link-boy suddenly, and waited while his customer searched and found a penny. Then, payment being made, he flickered off and was rapidly extinguished in the premature night.

'And where have you been, Nightingale?' asks Mr Paris severely.

'I come over all queer at Mr Greening's,' says Nightingale humbly; and means it with all his heart. He has managed to deposit the mysterious box under the counter without being seen, before presenting himself to his master.

Mr Paris looks closely, then resumes his glazed smile.

He believes his apprentice, having satisfied himself that he certainly *looks* queer.

'He was taken over queer at Greening's,' he tells Mrs Paris as they sit down to table.

Nightingale looks up from his plate apologetically – and sees Miss Lucinda staring at him in triumph. He tries, with his eyes alone, to make some sort of approach to her; but without the smallest success.

For the rest of the day he is given only light tasks; Mr Paris is not an unkindly man, when things are brought face to face with him; he is really concerned for his pale, listless-looking apprentice. He begins to wonder if he has been altogether wise in caging a country Nightingale . . . ?

Nightingale himself has similar thoughts; he dreads more than ever the coming of the night. Try as he might, he cannot imagine what terrible vengeance on his behalf has been concealed in the box. What if his master's daughter should be killed by it? That would turn him into a murderer!

The ugly Mr Greening and his weaselish apprentice haunt his mind like a pair of malicious spirits in a darkened room. He resolves he will do nothing with the box. He is quite set on that; he'll not raise a finger to provide either the light or the easel . . . Then, quite out of the blue, Mr Paris bids him carry the easel from the workroom into the shop, ready to display Job's frame which will soon be finished.

Nightingale's heart falters as fate comes in on Mr Greening's side.

'Candle in the window won't do us much good on a night like this,' says Mr Paris, looking out into the

deplorable weather. He glances back at his distinctly frightened and ill-looking apprentice, and then at the gloomy counter under which he is to sleep. 'But keep it going all the same. Leave the shutters down and let a little brightness inside for a change, Nightingale.'

Thoughtfully he turns the looking-glasses in the window so that they face inwards and reflect the candle quite strongly upon the empty easel in the shop.

Nightingale feels a sense of panic concerning the powers of Mr Greening as he watches the father unknowingly arranging matters conveniently for the striking down of his own daughter.

At last the apprentice is left alone. He fetches out the box, takes off its outer coverings and places it on the easel. There is only a thin lid between him and whatever the box contains. He has determined that he will look in it himself. The candlelight, multiplied by the looking-glasses, dances and glitters on the box. Nightingale reaches out a hand, trembling in every limb at what he is about to behold. Mr Greening and his apprentice rise up before his inner eye and scream warnings . . .

'Nightingale!'

It is *she*. She has opened the door and stands just within the room. Her eyes fall upon the easel and the covered object upon it. She sees the apprentice standing before it, pale as death.

'What have you got there?'

Nightingale withdraws the hand that had been about to uncover Mr Greening's gift.

'A – a sort of mirror, you might say,' he answers, helplessly repeating the words of the weaselish apprentice. To his horror, he hears, in his own voice, a reflection of the weasel's mocking tone.

Miss Lucinda hears it, too.

'Let me see it,' she says, and pushes him to one side.

He smiles in a dazed, glazed fashion, feeling that it is fate that has pushed him and not Miss Lucinda. She reaches out, but seeing his smile, hesitates.

'You've arranged this, haven't you?'

He does not answer; he does not need to.

'It's your revenge, isn't it?'

'Not mine,' mutters Nightingale, thinking of the ugly Mr Greening.

'You've put something vile in there,' says Miss Lucinda contemptuously. 'Some disgusting thing out of your own brain.'

She lowers her hand and Nightingale sighs with audible relief. She falls silent and Nightingale hangs his head in an effort to avoid her brilliant and penetrating eyes. Then he looks up and sees that once more she has raised her hand and now rests it upon the thin lid of the box.

'Your thoughts,' she says. 'They're here, aren't they? What do they amount to? A toad? A piece of filth? Something dead and rotting? Something so foul and degrading that it's best covered up? Let's see, Nightingale, once and for all, how mean and depraved an apprentice's mind and heart can be!'

She laughs, and before Nightingale can stop her, she lifts up the lid. Light streams into the box, and the lid falls with a clatter from her hand. Nightingale turns away in terror. He waits for some shriek or sound of death; but there is only silence. Fearfully he looks back. She has not moved. A terrible pallor has spread over her face; even her lips, for all their redness, have gone a greyish white. What horrible, deadly thing did Mr Greening hide in the box?

She breathes deeply as if suffering from an intolerable constriction; and the something so degrading that it should have been covered up, gazes back at her. Helplessly she looks, with pitiless clarity, upon – herself.

Mr Greening's box contains no more than a perfect mirror. Neither ripple, tarnish nor flaw interposes to alleviate the girl from the image that she herself has so monstrously described.

Her expression, halted by shock, has remained unchanged from the look she'd worn before. Every mark of scorn, contempt, lamed ambition and cruelty are bloodlessly plain. The very smile of deep pride – that had once lent her a sort of distinction – robbed of its colour, has become a dull sneer. The eyes, fixed on the bland surface of the glass, have lost all brightness, all penetration, and become as glass; glass eyes in a glass head . . .

Filled with guilt and fear, Nightingale approaches to see what it is she has seen. As he moves, she gives a low and anguished cry, which resembles, not so much a sound as a shudder made audible, for it is accompanied by a continuous, violent trembling.

She is mortally afraid that he will see what she has seen, that he will see her as she now sees herself. His countenance joins her as she watches it, examines it minutely with ever-increasing agony.

'But it's only glass!' says Nightingale, with gentle amazement.

'Only glass,' she repeats, finding in the apprentice's face nothing worse than relief and bewilderment. 'Quicksilver, lead and glass . . .'

'That's how they make mirrors, isn't it?' says Nightingale, as if persuading a child out of too strong a dream.

'They put lead, as thin as paper, on the glass and pour quicksilver over it,' she murmurs. 'I've watched it being done. My father once took me. I'll take you, if you like . . . some day . . . if you like . . .'

Nightingale moves closer. He cannot really help himself . . . For a moment, their faces are reflected together, then their joined breath mists the glass, obscures them and dissolves eyes, lips, cheeks and tears into a strange, double countenance, seen, as it were, in a glass brightly.

But the candlelight, reflecting busily off all the looking-glasses from the window, keeps catching at the corners of Nightingale's eyes so that he seems to be looking into the heart of a diamond.

He blinks and turns away, glancing, as he does so, from mirror to mirror, in each of which he sees his master's daughter. Sometimes he sees her in profile, sometimes just the coils of her golden hair, sometimes the curve of her cheek and the projecting edge of her lashes; and sometimes, as strange as the other side of the moon, her second profile ... He looks and looks, and as far as his eyes can see, his universe is filled with Lucindas ...

And she, at last abandoning her reflection to the eyes of another, follows his example and roams the angled

mirrors. Everywhere she sees him, but cannot, by reason of the confused architecture of light, make out for certain what it is he is gazing at. She looks and looks, and as far as her eyes can see, her universe is filled with Nightingales . . . and their song is suddenly sweet.

Outside, the fog piles up and rolls comfortably past the window of Mr Paris's shop; from somewhere in the invisible street, a gentleman curses as he trips over a lamplighter's ladder, and from every darkened corner come the link-boys' eager cries of:

'Light you home, mister! Light you home, ma'am!'

Moss and Blister

to Vivien

There they go, Moss and Blister, hurrying up Black-friar's Stairs and on through the dark streets, under a sky fairly peppered with stars as cold as frozen sparks. Up Coalman's Alley, across Bristol Street . . .

''appy Christmas, marm – and a nappy Christmas to you, miss!' bellowed a bellman, coming out of an ale-house and wagging his bell like a swollen brass finger.

'*For unto us a Child is born, unto us a Son is given!*' he hiccuped; and read out a little Christmas poem of his own composing while Moss and Blister stood stock still and listened. Then he held out his hand and Moss put a sixpence in it, for it was Christmas Eve, and Moss, who was a midwife, felt holy and important.

Ordinarily Moss was brisk and businesslike to a degree; but on this one night of the year she was as soft as butter and gave her services for nothing. She lived in hopes of being summoned to a stable and delivering the Son of God.

'It's written down, Blister,' she said to her apprentice,

after the bellman had weaved away. 'It's all written down. *Unto them that look for him shall he appear the second time.*'

Blister, a tall, thin girl with sticking-out ears and saucer eyes, who flapped and stalked after stubby Moss like a loose umbrella, said: 'Yus'm!' and looked frightened to death. Blister also had her dream of Christmas Eve and a stable; but it was not quite the same as Moss's. She dreamed that Moss would be delivering *her* of the marvellous Child.

Naturally she kept her ambition a deep secret from Moss, so that the dreamy frown that sometimes settled on her face led Moss to surmise that her apprentice was a deep one . . . Mostly these frowns came in the springtime, for Moss knew it would take nine months . . . which was one less than the toes on both her feet. At the end of every March she'd lie in her bed, waiting with ghostly urgency for Moss to appear beside her; for Moss had a gift like the angel of the annunciation. She could tell, long before it showed, if any female had a bun in the oven, a cargo in the hold or a deposit in the vault – depending on the trade concerned.

She'd stop dead in the street, fix her eye in a certain way upon some lightsome lass, dig Blister in the ribs, and follow the female to her home. Then she'd leave her card and everyone in the neighbourhood would know that a happy event was on the way. Truly, the sight of Moss, in her ancient cape that was green with rain and age, was as sure a sign of pregnancy as morning sickness or a passion for pickles.

But she never looked at Blister in that certain way; and every Christmas Eve Blister would grow frightened that someone else had been chosen to bear the glory of the world. The dreamy frown, but now tinged with apprehension and melancholy, settled on her face as she floundered on in Moss's wake.

'Make 'aste, marm!' shrieked out a link-boy, streaking his torch along a row of railings so that a fringe of fire fell down and iron shadows marched across the houses like the army of the Lord. 'Cat's 'avin' kittens!'

'There's a imp for impidence!' puffed Moss, shaking her fist and making as if to rush upon the hastily fleeing offender. 'Just let me catch 'im and I'll pop 'im back where 'e came from!'

'Just let *me* catch 'im!' screeched Blister, shaking her fist likewise, so that midwife and apprentice made a pattern in the street of wrath in two sizes.

Then Moss gave up and beckoned to Blister; there was no time to waste; they were needed in Glass House Yard where Mrs Greening's waters had broken and the whole household was having contractions in sympathy.

'D'yer fink it'll be the one?' panted Blister, swinging her heavy business bag from one hand to the other. 'You know – '*im* what's comin' for the second time?' Her voice trembled, and so did her lip.

'Nar,' said Moss. 'It's got to be in a stable, Blister. Ain't I told you that? There's got to be a donkey and three kings and wise men with frankincense and – and more.'

'Wot's frankincense?'

'It's a sort of fruit. Summat between a orringe and a pommygrunt,' answered Moss, who did not care to appear ill-informed.

Blister nodded. They really were pig-ignorant, the

pair of them; although why a pig, who knows where to find truffles and live the good life, should be put on a level with Moss and Blister, passes understanding. Moss didn't even know that the world was round, while Blister didn't know that China was a place as well as a cup. Moss's arithmetic – apart from counting out her fee, about which she was remarkably sharp – was confined to the natural proposition that one and one, coming together, can make one, or, sometimes, two – twins being the largest number she had ever been called upon to deliver. And Blister was even more ignorant than that.

Although she knew her trade in every particular, and could have delivered a baby as safely as kiss-your-hand, she'd no more idea of how the seed had been planted than she knew what happened to the River Thames after it went past Wapping. Moss had never seen fit to enlighten her. In Moss's view, all that Blister needed to know was how to get babies out; getting them in was no part of the trade. The nearest she ever came to telling Blister was at Christmastide when she went on, with a radiant smile, about a woman being with child of the Holy Ghost. This made Blister very frightened; she had nightmares of being confronted, when she least expected it, by something inexpressibly fierce in a sheet.

Presently they reached Glass House Yard, and there was Mr Greening's shop, leaking light and commotion at every joint. They began to cross the dark cobbles, when Moss cried out.

'Stop! Stop!' She halted in her tracks with her arms spread out so that her cape fell down like a pair of mildewy wings. Something had darkened her path.

'Black cat, Blister! Cross your fingers and think of wood – else the baby will be wrong way round!!'

Obediently Blister dropped her bag, crossed her fingers and emptied her mind of everything except a broomstick that stood behind Moss's kitchen door. It was the only wood she knew.

'Done it, mum.'

Moss heaved a sigh of relief and advanced upon the premises of Mr Greening.

'You can't be too careful,' she said, giving her famous double knock upon the door. 'Not where such 'appiness is at stake!'

'They're 'ere! They're 'ere! Thank Gawd you've come! Mr Greening – it's the midwife! Mrs Greening! It's all right now! Oh thank Gawd you're 'ere! They're all goin' off their 'eads! Is it always like this, marm?'

Mr Greening's apprentice, who was small and sharp like a weasel, and who nursed ambitions of becoming one of the family, was quite beside himself with anxiety and excitement as he admitted Moss and Blister through the trade counter that occupied the entrance of the establishment. 'They'll remember this,' he thought to himself as he took Moss's cape and offered to assist Blister with her bag. 'They'll remember how I give up me Christmas and worritted myself sick like a son!'

Mr Greening himself appeared. He was an ugly man with a nose like a warty old potato. He was a silverer of mirrors, which was an unusual trade for one of his un-lucky appearance.

'Thank God you've come!' he cried.

Next came the Greenings' two daughters, young
ladies of twelve and fourteen, and quite as ugly as their
father.

'Thank God you're here! We thought ma was going
to die!'

Then a maidservant looked in, and a neighbour's
wife, and *they* thanked God for Moss, so that Moss felt
deliciously holy all over. With a wave of her hand she
dispatched Blister upstairs to see how things were pro-
ceeding; then she went into the warm bright parlour to
receive whatever else of respect, gratitude and hospitality might be coming her way.

'This way, miss! Do let me carry yer bag. Gawd, it's
'eavy!' exclaimed the weaselish apprentice as he conducted Blister up the stairs and towards the room from
which Mrs Greening could be heard moaning and

peevishly inquiring where everyone had gone. 'Wotcher got in it, miss? The Crahn jewels?'

'Instryments,' said Blister. 'Knives and forksips and fings.'

'Gawd,' said Mr Greening's apprentice. 'It's a real business, ain't it?'

Blister smiled proudly and the weaselish one couldn't help reflecting that the saucer-eyed Blister was a raving beauty compared with the two Miss Greenings at whom he'd set his cap in the hopes of marrying one of them – he didn't care which – and inheriting the business.

'Make much money at it?'

'Not on Christmas Eve,' said Blister. 'We don't charge then.'

'Why ever not?'

'Ain't you 'eard? It's on account of the Son of God might be comin'. It's all written down.'

'I never 'eard of that one!'

'You're pig-ignorant, you are,' said Blister, loftily.

'No more'n you. 'ow would you silver a mirror?'

'Dunno. 'ow would yer deliver a hinfant arse first?'

'Send for you! What's yer name?'

'Blister. 's on account of me skin bein' all bubbly when I came out. What's your name?'

'Bosun. It's on account of me family bein' Bosuns.'

'I never 'ad a family. I was given to Moss when she delivered me. Sort of present. Moss took a fancy to me, called me Blister and brung me up.'

'Like 'er daughter?'

''prentice. She ain't got a daughter . . .'

Bosun nodded and, with an affable smile, stood aside for Blister to enter Mrs Greening's room.

The lady lay in her bed, weeping and groaning that all the world had abandoned her, that nobody cared any more and that she was going to die.

There was indeed some reason for this latter fear as she was advanced in years and had begun to believe herself past the age of child-bearing. Like Sarah of old when the messengers from God had crossed the plain of Mamre to tell Abraham that his wife was with child, Mrs Greening had laughed when Moss had called and left her card. She'd leaned behind the door and laughed at the stout little angel of the annunciation till the tears had run down her cheeks.

But then, as the days and weeks had gone by, she'd come to laugh on the other side of her face; for Moss had been right and the mirror-maker's wife did indeed 'have a little reflection in the glass'.

'I'm going to die,' moaned Mrs Greening, seeing that her visitor was only the midwife's gawky apprentice. 'It's true – it's true!'

'Yus'm,' said Blister, who had been taught there were two things in the world that there was no sense in arguing with: bad weather and a woman in labour.

She opened her bag and began to set out the instruments on a table. They were a ferocious assortment: scalpels, cruelly curved bistouries, probes, leathern forceps, scissors and a bone-saw that, from age and infirmity, had lost all but a few of its harsh teeth. Moss had picked them up, as she liked to call it, at various stages in her career when she'd attended in the presence of surgeons. She hadn't the faintest notion what they were for; the only instruments she actually used were her small strong hands and a pair of dressmaker's scissors she'd also picked up and which she kept in her pocket to cut the umbilical cord. Nevertheless she insisted that Blister always lay out the whole surgical armoury as she felt the sight of it gave her a real professional standing and the air of one who was not to be trifled with.

Mrs Greening, watching Blister's preparations, lost her fears in a terrified awe; dying was nothing beside what her imagination had suddenly proposed. Blister, sensing the lady's respect, felt proud; but at the same time she couldn't help wishing the weaselish apprentice outside the door could also behold her in her importance.

She'd been quite taken with Bosun and had been flattered by his admiration for the mystery of her craft.

'You must keep yer mouf shut, marm,' she said, loudly enough for Bosun to hear and be further impressed by her wisdom. 'Breeve froo yer nose.'

'Why must I do that?'

''case yer baby's born wivout sense or soul. Gets out froo yer mouf, marm.'

For the time being, Mrs Greening gave up groaning and shut her mouth.

'That's it, marm,' said Blister, and went to unlatch the window. 'Mustn't 'ave nuffink shut,' she said. 'Else yer labour will be 'ard as nails. Winders, doors, boxes, cupboards, drors . . . all got to be open. An' bockles, of course—'

'What?'

'Bockles – bockles! No stoppers or corks in 'em. Anyfink corked up corks up you, too.'

'Tell Bosun,' said Mrs Greening feebly.

But there was no need; Bosun had heard.

'Right away, Mrs G.! Don't you fret, marm! Bosun'll open everything!'

With a sound of thunder, Bosun was off, turning keys, lifting lids, opening bottles and dragging out crowded, obstinate drawers. 'They'll remember this,' he thought, 'when I comes to ask for the 'and of one of them ugly girls. They'll remember 'ow Bosun ran 'is feet off like a lovin' son!'

'Knots,' said Blister. 'Mustn't 'ave nuffink tied nor knotted. Twists you up, else. If you got a norse or a dawg, it's got to be untied, else the hinfant won't be able to get out.'

All these strange requirements, these pebbles of

magical wisdom that were laid up in Blister's head, had been gathered by Moss in her rollings among mothers and grandmothers whose memories stretched back to the beginnings of time. Moss had taken them all in, rejecting nothing, however far-fetched, and passed them on to her apprentice with the deep words: 'You can't be too careful; not where such 'appiness is at stake!'

'I think it's dead!' said Mrs Greening, in a sudden panic. 'I can't feel it any more! It's dead – it's dead!'

'Yus'm,' said Blister, and, drawing back Mrs Greening's bedclothes, bent down and laid her large, sticking-out ear to Mrs Greening's hugely swollen belly.

Now as no one was talking about Blister, her ears were as cold as ice.

'Mother of God!' shrieked Mrs Greening; and Blister started in pleased surprise to hear herself thus addressed.

'Yus'm?'

'The pain! The pain!'

Downstairs in the parlour, Moss was sipping port wine, which always imparted a rare skill to her fingers, and a brightness to her eyes.

'Never put the stopper on, sir,' she said reproachfully to Mr Greening; and gently, but firmly, she took the decanter into her own hands and refilled her glass. 'Nor clasp your 'ands nor cross your legs, else the baby'll never come.'

Mr Greening compressed his sensible lips and cast his eyes towards the ceiling. Nevertheless, he obeyed the

midwife's injunction. Even as he did so, everyone heard Mrs Greening shriek out, and directly after came Blister's shout:

'She's started! Come on up, marm! She's on the way!'

The mirror-maker stared down in bewilderment at his uncrossed knees and everyone else in the parlour looked terrified as if they'd just received an inkling of a mysterious web of laws in which they were all caught, like so many helpless flies. The neighbour's wife, who had been inclined to regard Moss's superstitions with contempt, now stared at the fat little midwife with a respect that bordered on dread. And so she should have done; for Moss knew very well what she was about, and was right to neglect nothing when such happiness was at stake.

Moss finished off her wine and rose to her feet.

'I'll call you,' she said, 'when it's over.'

She left the parlour and briskly mounted the stairs. Outside Mrs Greening's door, she came upon Bosun who had gone very white in the face as the cries and grunts from within increased in urgency.

'You must cover up all the mirrors,' she told him, 'else the baby will be born blind.'

Bosun nodded and prepared to fly at the midwife's bidding. She raised her hand.

'And put neither wood nor coal on the fire till the cord's cut; else the baby might be born dead.'

'I never knew, I never guessed there was so much to it, marm.'

'You can't be too careful,' said Moss, sombrely, 'where such 'appiness is at stake.'

Bosun fled. 'They'll remember this,' he thought. 'They'll remember 'ow Bosun was a real son to them!'

By the time he'd scoured the premises and covered up every last glimmer of reflecting silver and returned to his station outside the bedroom door, matters were far advanced. Panting and gulping, he listened . . .

''old 'er legs, Blister! Up a bit . . .'

'Yus'm.'

'Bear down, mother! Bear down wiv all yer might!'

'I can't! I can't!'

''old your breff when it comes on! 'old yer breff when you feel it pushin' . . .'

'It's burning me – it's burning me like fire!'

'Bear down agin, mother! Blister! Give 'er knees another shove! Push, mother! Push like ye'r rollin' a cart of 'ay!'

'I can't . . . I – I've no more strength!'

''old yer breff agin! Ah! I can see it! Luvly little thing! Ye'r all but crownin' now, mother!'

'No – no! I don't want to! It's going to kill me! Stop it!'

''eave ho! 'eave ho!'

But Mrs Greening was still reluctant to bring forth the little 'reflection in her glass', and she began to curse and swear in a way that made Bosun's toes curl up. He'd no idea his mistress knew such words, nor was so wild and abandoned a soul as she sounded.

''eave ho! 'eave ho! mother,' urged Moss; and there followed a most awesome grunting, as of stout hawsers straining when the full tide heaves a great vessel to tug against its moorings.

'Ugh! Ugh! Ugh!'

''eave ho! 'eave ho!'

'Ugh! Ugh! Ugh!'

'Don't let 'er go, Blister!'

'Yus'm.'

'There ain't nothing knotted anywhere, Blister?'

'Bosun!' screeched out Blister anxiously.

'Yes, miss?'

'Boot laces! Got 'em undone?'

Bosun looked down. His shoes were tightly laced – and double-knotted. Guiltily he bent down and tried to untie them. His fingers shook and trembled, but the knots defeated him. Mrs Greening moaned and groaned; Moss urged her to still greater efforts – and Bosun pulled and snapped his laces.

'Done it – done it, miss!' he shouted in triumph; and Mrs Greening gave a last mighty cry.

'Clever girl!' said Moss. 'Blister! Get me scissors out, there's a dear!'

'Yus'm.'

'Look what a luvly little thing it is! All its fingers and toes! Listen – listen! Ah! There it goes!'

Suddenly there came a fragile sound, so thin and winding that it scarcely seemed to make its way through the air. It was the sound of a voice, brand new, never before heard since the beginning of time.

'And I done it!' thought Bosun, looking down incredulously at his broken boot laces. 'Oh, they'll remember this when I comes to offer meself as their son!'

'Tell Mr Greening!' sighed the mother's exhausted, happy voice. 'I want Mr Greening to come . . .'

'Bosun!'

'Yes, miss?'

'Go tell 'em it's over and everyfing's all right! Tell Mr Greenin' to come on up an' 'ave a look at 'is wife an' son!'

'They'll remember this,' thought Bosun, flying down the stairs, 'when I'm their SON!'

The last word came out aloud, in a dismayed grunt and squeal. A son! But now they'd already got one!

In the twinkling of an eye the apprentice's ambitions tumbled as the tiny creature he himself had done so much to deliver safely, usurped his prospects. He saw it all. It would grow and grow and, sooner or later, come to lord it over him; Bosun would count for nothing; the newcomer would inherit the business . . .

'You got a son, Mr Greening,' he said, entering the expectant parlour and doing his best to keep the dismay out of his voice. 'You got a bruvver,' he said, gazing mournfully at the two ugly daughters. At least, he thought, he would no longer have to worry which of

them would be the least disagreeable to marry. It's an
ill wind, he reflected wryly, that don't blow at least
some good!

Everyone in the parlour exclaimed aloud with joy
and began hastening upstairs; while Bosun – passed-
over Bosun – went about fastening latches, closing doors
and corking up all the bottles with the vague, melancholy feeling that he was bolting the stable door after
the horse had gone. He looked down at his loosened
shoes. He sighed.

'And I'll even 'ave to buy meself new laces!'

He peered into the fire he'd just replenished and tried
to see castles in the coals. 'They've forgotten,' he
thought. 'They've forgotten all about Bosun now.' He
shifted a piece of coal to make a roof for what would

have been a fine mansion; but it fell through and the walls collapsed into blazing ruins. ''ow like life,' whispered Bosun. ''ow like life!'

'Bosun?'

'Yes, miss?'

Blister had come down; she looked flushed and disarranged from her recent efforts. Even her ears stuck out more than usual; like a pair of cupboard doors, thought Bosun, bitterly. He couldn't help regarding her as the part author of his misfortune.

'Mr Greenin' says you're to gimme a glass of port wine to drink 'is son's elf.'

'Yes, miss.'

'An' 'e says you're to 'ave one yerself.'

'I ain't thirsty,' said Bosun; but nevertheless he joined Blister. There was, after all, no law that could make him drink to the infant who had just done him out of his inheritance.

''ere's to seein' your face in the glass!' he said defiantly.

''ere's to the Son of God!'

'The son of Greening, you mean.'

Blister shook her head wisely.

'It's got to come in a stable, wiv' free kings an' a donkey and a special star.'

'That'll be the day!'

'It'll come; one Christmas Eve. It's all written down.'

'And will you be there to 'elp?'

'I'll be there,' said Blister, shutting her saucer eyes tightly and swilling down her wine. 'Me an' the 'oly Ghost.'

She swallowed and opened her eyes, and the two apprentices gazed at one another over the tops of their glasses: the one mournful, the other still full of hope. In one, ambition had fallen; in the other, it still remained in the skies.

'She ain't really such a bad looker,' thought Bosun. 'In a narrer glass you'd never see them ears!'

''ave another glass of wine!' offered Bosun, feeling distinctly less careful over his master's property than he would have done half an hour before.

'Yus!' said Blister, thrusting out her long, thin arm.

Bosun recharged the glasses and smiled somewhat crookedly.

''ere's to seein' *your* face in the glass!' said Blister, politely echoing her companion's toast.

'And 'ere's to the Son of God!' responded Bosun. They drank.

''ave—' began Bosun, when there came a loud knocking on the street door. Bosun frowned and put down his glass. ''elp yourself,' he said. And then added broodingly, 'We all got to 'elp ourselves, miss.'

He left the parlour and clattered through the shop. Blister felt a gust of cold night air come sweeping in as the street door was opened; she shivered. Bosun returned.

'It's for you. Midwife wanted. In a 'urry. 'ow did they know you was 'ere?'

'We allus tell a neighbour in Glastonbury Court. They 'ave to know where to find us. Moss!' screeched Blister.

'What is it, Blister?'

'Anuvver call! In a 'urry!'

'Whereabouts?'

Blister looked inquiringly at Bosun.

'Said it were in Three Kings Court.'

'Free Kings Court, Moss!'

'*Three Kings?*' Moss's voice took on an edge of excitement. 'What 'ouse?'

'New Star public 'ouse,' said Bosun.

'The Noo Star, Moss!' howled Blister.

'The New Star? The New Star?' repeated Moss, from upstairs. 'Christmas Eve, three kings and a new star? Blister! Come an' fetch yer instryments! Blister! It might be the one! 'urry, girl, 'urry!'

Blister and Bosun stared at one another. Curiosity and excitement filled the heart of one apprentice; apprehension and dread clutched at the other.

Could it really be the one? thought Blister. Never!

Three kings and an inn called the New Star weren't enough. It had to be more than that. Partly relieved, she ran upstairs to collect her instruments.

'Carry yer bag, miss?' offered Bosun impulsively, as Blister came down again in the wake of the fat and trembling Moss.

'Wot? All the way to Free Kings Court? Won't they miss you 'ere?'

'Not now they got a son,' said Bosun, bitterly. 'Besides,' he went on, brightening a little, 'if it's '*im* – you know, the one what we drunk to – I'd like to see 'im. Wouldn't want to miss 'im. It'd be summat to remember all right.'

'It won't be 'im,' said Blister, thrusting out her lower lip. 'It can't be 'im. It needs more'n free kings and a star . . .'

''urry, Blister! 'urry!' Moss was already in the street. 'What if it's reely 'im an' we're too late?'

There they went, Moss and Blister, hurrying by star-light, with Bosun clanking the bag of instruments and keeping a watch for footpads and other demons of the night. They hastened up Water Street and into Ludgate Hill . . .

'It's got to be in a stable!' panted Blister.

''appy Christmas, 'appy Christmas!' called out a pair of watchmen on Fleet Bridge who were warming themselves before a brazier of glowing coals that threw up their faces in a ruddy comfort amid the empty fields of the night.

'Look, Blister, girl! Shepherds abidin' ... and the glory of the Lord shinin' all round 'em! Make 'aste, make 'aste! I reely think it might be the night!'

But it took more than that to convince Blister. She shook her head so violently that tiny drops of salt water flew out of her saucer eyes.

'It ain't the night! It ain't!' she muttered, as they passed Temple Bar and came into the Strand. 'There's got to be frankincense and – and more!'

'What's frankincense?' asked Bosun, ready to come upon it at any moment if only he knew what to look for.

Blister did not answer; she was in no mood to tempt fate. Moss put on a spurt of speed and scuttled on ahead. Still shaking her head, Blister stalked after, into Southampton Street and Covent Garden. Bosun, burdened with the heavy bag, came panting up beside her.

'And – and there's got to be a donkey,' mumbled Blister, putting yet another obstacle in the way of Moss's heart's desire, 'and a wise man from the east.'

As they drew near Three Kings Court, her great saucers were awash with new tears. She bit her lip and clenched her fists; and then, wickedness of wickedness, she secretly knotted a corner of her cape and vowed to keep her fingers crossed against the coming, that night, of the Son of God. It had to be her, and her alone, who was to be got with child of the Holy Ghost. She peered furtively up to the stars.

''ere I am,' she whimpered. 'Blister! It's me you're lookin' for! Me! Down 'ere. Me wiv the big ears ...'

Thus Blister, in her bottomless ignorance, strove with all her might and main to prevent the second coming on that Christmas Eve. That such an event would mark

the end of the world's misery meant nothing to Blister. What would be the good of it? In the middle of all the happiness she would have remained the one black spot of woe; and made all the darker by the thoughtless brightness all around. Moss would forget her in the excitement; Moss would be on her knees before a stranger, and Blister would be out in the cold . . .

At last they came to Three Kings Court where a single lantern lit up the frontage of the New Star Inn. Despite its name, the New Star was the oldest building in the court. It was left over from the days when Covent Garden had been a convent garden and had supplied the palace of Westminster with fruit and vegetables. Since then, however, tall tenements had come crowding in, imprisoning the New Star and taking away its pleasant garden. Only the coaching yard remained to mark its former glory; but even that was a mockery as no vehicle could possibly have gained entry to the court through the narrow passage that was all that the greedy builders had seen fit to leave as a way in.

There was, in point of fact, a bulky, old-fashioned coach still standing in a corner of the cobbled yard. It was a dreamy, melancholy sight that suggested a great journey abandoned, or a faithful love discarded and forgotten in the haste of new prospects. For a time it had been used as a trysting place; but when the roof had rotted and the seats decayed, it had become a playground for children . . .

Under the arch that formed the entrance to the yard stood a grimy, oil-smelling lamplighter who lived nearby. It was he who was holding the lantern and swinging it, turning the night into an earthquake of sliding shadows.

'She's in there,' he said to Moss.

'Where?'

'In the stable.'

Moss turned to Blister and Bosun. Her face was ecstatic.

'It's no good!' whispered Blister. 'There's got to be a donkey, too!'

They passed under the arch and crossed the yard. The lamplighter followed them, and his swaying lantern was reflected in the windows of the derelict coach so that it seemed, for a moment, that the abandoned

vehicle had come to life and was inhabited by a procession of spirits bearing candles . . .

The innkeeper's wife, hearing the footsteps on the cobbles, hastened out to meet the midwife.

'We wouldn't have known a thing about it,' she explained. 'She came in so quiet. It was only on account of her beast braying out that gave her away. And then we came out and found her . . .'

'Her beast?'

'She came on a donkey. It's in the stable now, eating its head off—'

'A donkey? A donkey! Gawd! Did you 'ear that, Blister?'

Blister heard. 'There's got to be a wise man,' she moaned softly.

'She's some sort of gipsy,' went on the innkeeper's wife. 'She's as dark as a nut. Come up from Kent, we fancy, selling apples. They thieve 'em out of barns down there, and travel into London on their donkeys like regular apple-sellers. She must have been took short in the Strand. She was squatting in the old coach when we found her. At first we thought she was just poorly ... so we took her into the stable as we'd got no rooms in the house at the moment. Then we saw what it was. She's very near her time . . .'

Although the innkeeper's wife tried to be casual and off-hand in her account, it was plain that she, no less than Moss, was moved by the strange and prophetic nature of the circumstance. Perhaps all this had been in her mind when she and her husband had decided to move the gipsy into the stable? Perhaps this is the way prophecies are meant to be fulfilled? *Seek and ye shall find; knock, and it shall be opened unto you.*

Two lamps, that had once lit the ancient coach on its way, shed their light now over the stall where the gipsy had found refuge in her distress, and a bucket of burning coals had been placed in a swept corner to give some warmth in the freezing night. The sight thus illumined was old and strange, full of mysterious shadows and still more mysterious light. There was the donkey, half emerging from the gloom and bowing its gentle head to nibble at the straw on which its mistress lay. Further back, half hidden by the wooden partition, stood the innkeeper and two or three travellers who had been putting up for the night. The dim light rendered their faces intent and profound . . .

'We've not managed to get a word out of her,' confided the innkeeper's wife. 'That we can understand, that is. She gabbled away in her own lingo when we took her out of the coach; but as soon as she saw we meant her no harm, she buttoned up her lip and she's been quiet as a mouse ever since.'

The gipsy was dark, brown as a nut. Her hair was black and was braided cunningly over her ears so that her oval face seemed to have been laid in a basket o black straw. Her eyes were as black as her hair and fixed themselves on Moss with a look that was at once suspicious and defiant. Only the drops of sweat that stood upon her high forehead betrayed that she was in any difficulty or pain.

'It's very unusual,' murmured one of the travellers, 'for any of her race to be abandoned at such a time. She must be an outcast of some description . . .'

'This gentleman seems to know a thing or two,' said the innkeeper's wife softly. 'He's what you might call a wise man.' As she said this, she gave a curious smile and a little nod to Moss. Blister wept; she stood alone before the inexorable power of fate.

Moss, her joints crackling like gunfire, knelt down beside the gipsy. Reverently she laid a hand, first on the woman's brow and then on her rusty black gown through which she strove to feel the motions of the child within. She looked up at Blister and nodded. Dully, Blister took her bag from Bosun and began to lay out her instruments on the straw.

The gypsy watched the preparations impassively, and

then transferred her gaze to Blister herself. Hastily Blister looked away. She dreaded that the woman, full of the mysterious gifts of her race, would be able to spy out the devil of jealousy that dwelt in Blister's soul.

The gipsy frowned, and bit on her red, red lip. Moss, observing this, drew in her breath sharply.

'Go see nothing's locked nor tied nor stopped up,' she murmured to Blister. 'I think 'e's comin' and we must make 'is way straight, like it says.'

Blister swallowed and retreated from the stall.

'I'll 'elp!' offered Bosun excitedly. He attempted to press Blister's hand under cover of darkness, but Blister shrank away . . .

'The donkey!' burst out Bosun, coming up upon

Blister suddenly. 'You forgot it! But no matter – I untied 'im!'

Blister stared at the weaselish apprentice with misery. He departed.

'There was a bit of old 'arness,' he said, appearing beside Blister again, ''angin' on a 'ook. I unbuckled it!'

Blister clenched her fists and the weasel scuttled busily off.

'There was an ol' bottle in the corner . . . I took the cork out! Don't you worrit, miss! I'll do what's needful . . . for the sake of '*im*!!'

Blister moaned.

'There was a copper pan polished so's you could see yer face in it. But I covered it up!'

Blister snarled, and Bosun, mistaking the sound for anxiety, reached out to comfort Blister.

'Miss – miss! There's a knot got into yer cape! 'old still and I'll undo it. There—'

Helplessly Blister submitted; she dared not let it be known what was in her heart.

'Blister! Come quick!'

Moss's voice was summoning her. She stared wildly towards the stall. The innkeeper and the travellers had moved back, out of decency and respect. A glow seemed to rise up from where the gipsy lay. Suddenly this glow became fiercely bright!

'I just put a bit of wood on the fire,' murmured the innkeeper's wife, 'to keep her warm.'

'Never do that!' squealed Bosun. 'That were wrong!' He rushed inside the stall and, burning his fingers, snatched the brand from the burning bucket and doused it in a barrel of water that stood nearby.

He smiled at Blister as she entered the stall.

'I 'opes,' he said, sucking his injured fingers, 'that 'e remembers this when we all come to be judged.'

Thereupon Bosun retired to the darkest part of the stable, where, with the innkeeper and the travellers, he awaited the birth of the saviour.

'Blister!'

'Yus'm?'

'Down 'ere! What the matter wiv you, girl? 'old the lady's knees. Gently – gently, girl! Remember what she might be! Oh my Gawd! She's all but crownin' and not a word nor a cry! It's a mirricle, all right!'

Blister, leaning forward and pressing on the gipsy's bent knees, put her face close and breathed fiercely:

'Were it the 'oly Ghost? Tell us – tell us!'

The gipsy's dark eyes widened and swam with moisture.

'Blister!'

'Yus'm?'

'What are you on at? Don't fret 'er! It's comin'! I – I can see 'is 'ead! It's 'im all right! It must be! 'e's *shinin*'!'

Bosun, in the shadows, heard the midwife's rapturous cry. The coming of the saviour instantly produced in his mind thoughts of a world where apprentices were level with their masters, where there was no toil to blunt the nights and days.

Moss thought of herself in a stained-glass window, offering the Son of God to the black-haired Queen of Heaven; while Blister, her apprentice, saw herself cast into the outer darkness, despised and rejected alike of the Holy Ghost and Moss and all mankind.

She glared, with fearful desperation, into the gipsy's eyes. She pretended to yawn, stretching wide her mouth. The gipsy looked suddenly frightened; she tried to clench her teeth against the awful power of Blister's example. An expression of terrified pleading came into her eyes as she strained. Blister was the devil, encouraging her to lose her child's soul through her open mouth! A great shudder convulsed her and she shook her head from side to side.

'Blister – Blister, my love!' sobbed Moss. 'That it should be us . . . together . . . on this night! Oh Blister, I knew, when I 'eld you in me arms, that you and me would do summat wonderful! Oh Blister! That were a blessed night when you was born!'

As she heard these words, Blister's heart lifted up. It had been a blessed night when she'd been born! She shut her mouth, and the gipsy bestowed on her a smile of the most wondrous radiance.

'Scissors, Blister! Where's me scissors? Quick, girl! What are you at?'

Bosun, staring towards the stall, believed he saw a radiance rising up as the glorious new life began. Then came the cry, like a thread of gold ... Everyone pressed forward eagerly.

'Oh Blister!' cried Moss, her voice shaking. 'Oh Blister! We wasn't worthy after all! It – it ain't 'im! It – it's a girl!'

Hopes raised foolishly, settled into ashes. The travellers went back to their rooms and the gipsy nursed her child while her donkey nodded and nibbled. The innkeeper's wife, rueful of countenance, bade the midwife farewell, and the old coach in the yard looked deader than ever as Moss, Blister and Bosun passed it by.

'If only,' said Bosun to Blister, 'they'd been the other way round. If only there'd been a girl at Mr Greening's and a boy 'ere! What a night that would 'ave been, eh?'

He sighed and pondered on how nearly he and the world had come to being saved.

'If only it 'ad been a boy!' sighed Moss, sniffing and dabbing her eyes.

'We'd never 'ave 'ad to work again,' said Bosun.

'There'd be no more dyin', said Moss.

'There'd be no more rainin' on Sundays,' said Bosun.

'There'd be no more damp winters,' said Moss. 'And no more growin' old.'

'There'd be strawberries all the year round,' said Bosun; 'growin' in the streets.'

'We'd all be wed,' said Moss; 'wiv never a death to part us.'

'We'd all be beautiful,' said weaselish Bosun. 'There wouldn't be a ugly face anywhere.'

He glanced at Blister, who was gazing up to the stars. Blister alone was neither mournful nor full of regrets. She was smiling, a strange, secret smile. She had not

been rejected, either of the Holy Ghost, or Moss, or mankind. She *had* been visited; she knew it. She smiled and smiled at the stars. Bosun continued to watch her and found her mysterious and quite heart-catching. Blister, feeling his scrutiny, looked into his eyes.

'All we needed was a boy,' sighed Moss.

'All we needed was a boy,' repeated Blister; and the two apprentices – the one like a beanpole, the other like a weasel – continued to gaze into each other's eyes.

''appy Christmas!' called the lamplighter, who still stood under the archway that led out into Three Kings Court. '*For unto us a Son is born!*'

'It were a girl,' said Moss sadly. 'We needed a boy.'

'But I got a boy,' murmured Blister.

'You got a boy,' agreed Bosun, and took her by the hand.

There they go, Moss, Blister and Bosun, hurrying through the dark streets.

'Moss!' called out Blister. 'It were *'im*, after all.'

Moss turned and looked back at Blister and then at Bosun. She smiled and nodded.

'In a manner o' speakin', dear,' she said. 'In a manner o' speakin'.'